D0309762

# RESIN

www.penguin.co.uk

For more information on Ane Riel and her
books, see her website at www.aneriel.dk

# RESIN

## ANE RIEL

*English translation by Charlotte Barslund*

Doubleday

LONDON · TORONTO · SYDNEY · AUCKLAND · JOHANNESBURG

TRANSWORLD PUBLISHERS
61–63 Uxbridge Road, London W5 5SA
www.penguin.co.uk

Transworld is part of the Penguin Random House group of companies
whose addresses can be found at global.penguinrandomhouse.com

Penguin
Random House
UK

First published in Great Britain in 2018 by Doubleday
an imprint of Transworld Publishers

A CIP catalogue record for this book
is available from the British Library.

ISBNs 9780857525451 (cased)
9780857525468 (tpb)

Typeset in 12/15 pt Bembo by Jouve (UK), Milton Keynes
Printed and bound in Great Britain by Clays Ltd, Elcograf S.p.A.

Penguin Random House is committed to a sustainable
future for our business, our readers and our planet. This book
is made from Forest Stewardship Council® certified paper.

MIX
Paper from
responsible sources
FSC® C018179

1 3 5 7 9 10 8 6 4 2

# RESIN

# Liv

The white room was completely dark when my dad killed my granny. I was there. Carl was there too, but they never noticed him. It was the morning of Christmas Eve and it had started snowing, but we didn't get a proper white Christmas that year.

Back then everything was different. It was before Dad's stuff started taking up so much space that we couldn't get into the living room. And before Mum grew so big that she couldn't get out of the bedroom, but it was after they had reported me dead, which got me out of going to school.

Or maybe it was earlier? I'm not very good at remembering when things happen, I get them muddled up. The first few years of your life feel like they'll never end. The lady tells me it's because when you try something for the first time, it makes a big impression on you, and those impressions take up a lot of space, she says.

There was definitely a lot going on in my life back then, and I was doing a lot of things for the first time. Like watching my granny die.

So anyway, our Christmas tree was hanging from the ceiling. There was nothing new about that. Dad used to hang stuff from the ceiling so he could cram as much into the living room as possible. He'd stack our presents underneath it, so we always hoped he'd bring home a small tree.

That year the tree must have been quite small because there was room for very big presents underneath it. One of them was an amazing go-kart which Dad had built in his workshop. Mum had made red cushions for the seats. Mum and Dad always made our presents. Back then I didn't know that other people's children got presents bought from shops. I barely knew that other people had children or that they got presents. It never bothered us. Carl and I were just pleased to get something, and we loved Mum and Dad. It's true there were times when Carl got a bit annoyed with them, but he could never say why.

So what was new about this Christmas was that my granny had just died. We hadn't tried that before, and neither had she, obviously. She certainly looked a bit shell-shocked, sitting there in the green armchair, staring up at the tree, not blinking. I think she was looking at a brown paper heart I made all on my own. She taught me to weave paper hearts before she said all those things to Dad, those things which she probably shouldn't have said.

We thought she should be with us round the tree that evening before her send-off, and she had to have her present, of course. OK, so only me and Dad thought that. And mostly me. Mum only gave in because I kept pestering her.

My granny's feet were on the footstool, I remember, probably because I was sitting on the floor right opposite her. Her purple tights were so thin I could see her knickers through them, and her brown lace-up shoes smelled sort of sweet, like some kind of waterproofing. They were brand new and she had bought them in a shop on the mainland, she told me. She was also wearing a grey skirt, a red blouse and a scarf with white seagulls on it, clothes I found at the bottom of her case. It was me who had insisted on dressing her up nicely for Christmas. Her sitting there in her nightie would have been all wrong.

After that Christmas, no one ever sat in the green armchair again. Soon, we simply couldn't.

It was covered in too much stuff.

As my granny couldn't take the newspaper wrapping off her present, I was allowed to do it. At first I thought Dad had made her a go-kart too, because her present was another long wooden box on wheels, but it turned out he'd made her a coffin. With no steering wheel or red cushions. And no lid. It didn't need a lid, he said. The only thing inside it was the pillow she'd been smothered with that morning.

When we'd put my granny in her coffin – with her head on top of the pillow this time rather than underneath it – Dad wheeled her out of the back door, around the house, past the log pile and out to the field behind the barn. Carl and I followed in the go-kart. I did the pushing, as usual, or we would have got nowhere. Mum followed behind. She always was a slowcoach.

It was pitch black, but we were used to moving about in the darkness out where we lived. The sky must have been thick with clouds that Christmas Eve because I couldn't see a single star; we could barely make out the forest that surrounded the house and the fields. It had been windy that morning, but nothing stirred now and the earlier snow had melted. Christmas seemed to have made up its mind to be quiet and dark.

We set my granny alight using firelighters, newspaper and the extra-long matches we'd been told never to play with but Carl did anyway. We took off her shoes first, of course. They were brand new and waterproofed.

It wasn't long before the heat forced us to step away. Soon the flames were so bright the water trough at the back of the yard emerged from the darkness and we could make out the low scrub at the edge of the wood. When I looked around, I saw my own shadow dancing on the barn wall behind me, and I could see Mum and Dad very clearly in the glow from the fire. They were holding hands.

I looked again at my burning granny with her white hair and my stomach did a somersault.

'Does it really not hurt her?' I asked.

'No, don't you worry,' Dad said. 'She doesn't feel a thing. She's not here any more.'

I was standing up in the go-kart and could still see my granny in her coffin, so his answer seemed a bit strange. Then again, I always believed whatever Dad said with all my heart. He knew everything. It was him who told me that you don't feel pain in the dark. The fish at the bottom of the sea, say, they didn't feel it when they bit on our hooks, and the rabbits didn't feel a thing when they got caught in our traps at night. 'Darkness takes the pain away,' Dad always said. 'And we only ever take the rabbits we need.' Which was why good people like us only went hunting at night.

Besides, the fact that my granny didn't utter a sound as she burned was all the proof I needed. She was always one to cry foul if she got hurt or if something didn't go her way. I've never heard anyone scream as loud as her that morning when a crate of tinned tuna came down on her head. She could get really cross.

She was still smouldering when we checked on her the next morning. Or checked on what was left of her, I guess I should say, because there wasn't a lot. A part of me was sad that she was gone because living with her was nice sometimes. Her pancakes were yummy.

When I popped by later that day there was nothing left but a bit of dark soil and singed grass. Dad said he'd cleared up and buried her. He never told me where.

Later, I often wondered if Dad did the right thing when he smothered her with that pillow. But he insisted that he had. Otherwise, things would have got much worse.

And my granny didn't protest when he did it. She just flopped about on the bed a bit until she was completely dead – a bit like a fish choking on air in the bottom of our dinghy. That was why we bashed them on their heads – so they wouldn't suffer. After all, none of us is meant to suffer.

Luckily, it was completely dark in my granny's bedroom early that morning on Christmas Eve, so being killed couldn't possibly have hurt her – or that was what I thought at the time. Anyway, it was quick because Dad pushed down hard. Selling Christmas trees, carrying planks, lugging things around and making furniture makes you strong.

Perhaps even I could have done it; he always said that I was really strong for my age, especially for a girl.

★

We lived on the Head, a small island beyond a bigger one. We were the only people living there, and we managed all on our own.

The Head was connected to the main island by a narrow strip of land known as the Neck. Like I said, I'm not good with times and dates, but Dad used to say it took just under half an hour if you walked fast to get from our house and across the Neck to the nearest clump of houses, and then fifteen minutes to reach Korsted, the biggest town on the island. I thought Korsted was huge, but my granny told me it was very small compared to the towns on the mainland. The thought of so many people in one place frightened me. I didn't feel safe around strangers. You never could tell with them, Dad always said. And you should never let yourself be taken in by their smiles.

The one good thing about the people down on the main island was that they had everything we needed.

Seeing as Dad didn't like leaving the Head at night very much now, it was mostly me who fetched things for us. Dad taught me how to do it a long time ago. But I preferred it before, when we went out together.

The two of us used to set off in the pickup truck, usually in the middle of the night when other people were fast asleep. We always found a good place to hide the truck, then we would sneak around and find things in barns and outhouses and sometimes in living rooms and kitchens and other places. Once, we crept into the bedroom of a woman who was so drunk we were able to take her duvet. Afterwards I wondered what she thought when she woke up and found it was gone. Dad told me he saw her in Korsted high street the next day. She looked a bit confused, but who could blame her? It was a goose-down duvet; she'd been left a lot of money, he said. Perhaps she thought it just flew away?

Mum got the goose-down duvet and I took her old duvet – one Dad had traded for a very fine meat press earlier that year. It was filled with duck down. A few months later we got the meat press back from the barber; he was never meant to keep it. The barber and his wife were asleep on the second floor, and the kitchen, where the meat press was, was on the ground floor. They hadn't even locked the back door. It was easy peasy lemon squeezy. Back then I believed that the barber was completely OK with us turning up and taking our things – or his things, or whoever's they were. His wife always reeked something awful; you could smell her all the way down in the kitchen. If I was the barber, I'd have wanted someone to take her rather than the meat press. Dad said the smell was perfume.

Mum's duck-down duvet reeked of the barber's wife for a long time, but when it was handed down to me it smelled mostly of Mum, thank God, not really of perfume any more and definitely not of duck. But Mum's new goose-down duvet stank of alcohol. Mum never drank anything stronger than coffee with cream, and at the end she drank only water from the pump; but I'll get to that part later.

Dad was brilliant at easing open doors and windows. His

dad had taught him, he told me. I never met Grandad, but I know that his name was Silas. Dad taught me too and I practised like mad in his workshop on some of the doors and windows we found. There were plenty at the junkyard down on the main island, and we piled up as many as we could on the back of the pickup truck. I can't understand why people would throw out things like that. You can always repair them – and you can open and close them and play with them.

We avoided houses that had new doors because they were difficult to open if people decided to lock them. Luckily there weren't many of them around. And if we couldn't get inside the house, there was usually a barn or an outhouse, and we'd find something to take there. Once we took a pig. We were short of a pig, and the farmer had so many he couldn't possibly eat all of them himself. I remember wondering why it didn't squeal; it wasn't even scared when Dad picked it up. But then again, he did have a way with animals. All animals. He was also very good at killing them so they didn't feel a thing. It was just another way of being kind to animals, he said.

When the time came for me to go off on my own, I didn't feel very confident to begin with. Especially because it very nearly went wrong on my last trip with Dad. We found a couple of long, rusty iron girders on the roadside and slid them up on the bed of the pickup truck, but when we drove around a corner in some village one of them hit a wall and made a huge racket. The lights came on in a few houses, but at the last minute Dad turned down a dirt track and we hid behind a hedge so no one saw us. The next day we lugged the iron girders upstairs; we could just about fit them along the corridor. You needed to watch your step after that, or you'd stub your toe on them.

There was another time where we were nearly caught, but that was my fault. I stepped on a hubcap in the plumber's garage by accident. I hid in a corner and held my breath when I heard the plumber open the door. If his cat hadn't jumped on him right then, he'd have turned on the light and spotted me. Instead he snapped at the cat: 'Is that you making all that noise? Get in here.'

When I came out of the garage, Dad was ashen-faced. He was waiting round the back and heard everything, but he didn't know about the cat.

But I soon found out there were some advantages to going off without Dad. I was smaller and faster, and I'd learned to move as quiet as a mouse. I walked or ran because I wasn't big enough to drive the pickup truck and I didn't like riding my bike. And I was much better at seeing in the dark than Dad. 'You need to be like the owl,' he often said, and I was, though I couldn't fly or turn my head round the back of my neck, even though I practised really hard, till I realized I'd never be any good at it. Carl tried as well, of course he did. He had a little more success.

Mum didn't say very much. I don't think she really wanted us to go out at night, but she liked the things we came back with. Especially the food from the pub kitchen.

★

One of the first things I remember from life on the Head is the smell of fresh resin: the funny tickling in my nose, the sticky feeling in the palm of my hand and Dad's calming voice telling me about the sap inside the tree. It was a strange sap, he said, because it could protect against attack, heal wounds *and* preserve small dead animals for ever and ever. I remember seeing an ant crawl up the bark of a tree, find a way around the gooey, golden drops and disappear inside a crack, only to come out again a bit further up. Upwards and onwards.

Later I would whisper to the bleeding trees that their wounds would soon heal because resin was their healer and protector. The trees were my friends.

And the ants were our mutual acquaintances. They were always there, small, steely creatures finding a way. Up the trees, down the trees, through the grass, across the yard, through the kitchen, up into the cupboard, down into the honey, through the living room, back home to the anthill. Usually they were dragging food or something that seemed useless – and sometimes a dead fellow ant.

I'm not sure if other people would call the trees behind our house a real forest. How many trees does it take to make a forest? But to Carl and me it was a forest, an enormous one. No, it was more than that. It was a never-ending world of smells and sounds and life which melted somewhere far away into a landscape of singing larks and heather and lyme grass that then merged into the sand, that merged into the water, that continued into an endless sea.

But it was some time before I found out about the heather and the sea. In the beginning there was just *the tree*; this one bleeding tree and the clever ant that avoided the sticky gold that could have suffocated it.

Later I noticed other trees: the spruces bending their fan-shaped branches towards the earth as if they wanted to hear what it was whispering to them. Spruces always seemed so sad, and though some of them grew incredibly tall, they continued to reach longingly down to the place from which they'd grown. Pines were completely different. They were dense and strong with their bristling needles and bursting cones, and I often got the feeling that they couldn't care less about the earth. I'm sure they were gazing at the sky and, who knows, they might happily fly away, if they could find a way of taking off from the forest floor. Though I like to think they would come back eventually. After all, they belonged on the Head, just like me.

And then there were the rustling trees. They would hide between the conifers with their slim, silver trunks topped with garlands of green leaves – small, spiky hearts that tingled like music in the wind. I loved that sound so much that I would sit under a rustling tree and wait for the wind to blow. I remember how frightened I was when one day the leaves suddenly started falling and scattering on to the ground around me. I sat in a sea of lost hearts. I tried sticking them back on to the branches – the lower branches, because I wasn't very tall – but however hard I tried, more and more leaves dropped. I didn't know what to do until I managed to get Dad's attention and he explained everything to me.

Ever since that day the forest became my favourite place because I had learned that everything comes back, that nothing ever goes away for good. That one colour replaces another, going from light green to dark green to flame red to golden brown to the darkest black before turning into mulch. That the earth had to eat in order to push new life into the light. That darkness replaced the light, and the light replaced the darkness. That the hearts would grow back.

Today I think Dad was happiest when he was surrounded by nature. He could breathe freely. We've never had as much fresh air and daylight as we had back then, and I'm sure that he got sunshine in his tummy just like me when we lay on our backs on the forest floor and watched the birds in the treetops. I knew every kind of birdsong before Mum taught me the alphabet song.

I wonder now if it was all that fresh air that kept Dad alive. That and all the light. Perhaps you can store it inside yourself to use later, just like you can keep memories in your head – and stacks of crispbread and crackers in the pantry, and umbrellas and hubcaps and record players in the kitchen, and hose clamps and nets and tinned food in the bathroom, and rolls of material and iron girders and fertilizer and petrol cans and newspapers and carpets in the corridor, and engine parts and sprung mattresses and bicycles and puppet theatres and violins and poultry feed in the living room, and towels and aquariums and sewing machines and wax candles and piles of books and biscuits in the bedroom, and a stuffed elk head in the room next to it, and cassette tapes and duvets and sand bags and foil trays and sacks of salt and paint pots and basins and teddies and children in a big old skip?

Even I can hear that it sounds weird when I say it like that, but that was how we lived. In time I learned we weren't like other people.

Dad was *definitely* not like other people.

Mum knew it too. I'm about to start reading the letters she hid for me in a slim green file. 'To Liv', it says on it.

That's my name. Liv.

I'm not going to read all of them at once. I don't like the thought of them running out, so I'm only going to read one at a time. I have lots of time, that's what the lady says.

*Dear Liv*

*I'm putting this letter first. The others you can read in whatever order you please. I'm not sure there even is any order. But I want you to read this one first.*

*I've never had the courage to tell you all the things I wanted to and, as my voice disappeared, I lost the ability. I never lost the need to tell you, though. But I can write and you can read – I've made sure of that – and one day you might read my thoughts here. Should that day come, I hope that you will be old enough to understand.*

*I've already written some longer letters for you, and there are also shorter ones; some notes too, my thoughts. I'm not sure how many letters there will be in the end. Or what the end will be.*

*I don't know whether to call our life a fairy tale or a horror story. Perhaps it's a bit of both? I hope that you can see the fairy tale.*

*I'm hiding this file from your dad; it's for the best. If I slip it in between the edge of the bed and the mattress, and cover it with a blanket, no one can see it, and in that way it will always be close when I have something to tell you.*

*It has become harder for me to reach. I'm so heavy now that I can barely turn over. And I hurt everywhere. But I won't ever give up writing to you, my darling girl.*

*Please forgive me if the contents of my letters seem chaotic. But I suppose you're used to navigating chaos so perhaps you'll understand everything in that way that you have. Perhaps you'll understand your dad too.*

*Perhaps you already do.*

*You need to know that I love him. You also need to know that he might kill me one day. If he does, I'll understand that, Liv.*

*All my love,*
*Mum*

# Jens Horder's Story

Once upon a time Liv's father was known as the most handsome man on the island, but over the years it grew increasingly hard to see why. Not only because his hair and beard grew wild and straggly, but also because it eventually became difficult to see him at all – not just behind the beard, but behind all the stuff piling up around him. No one had ever thought Jens would end up wreaking such havoc.

People on the island had always known him. That is to say, they had always known who he was. They would see him when he drove through Korsted in his ancient pickup truck. People of a certain age, and that was most people on the island, knew it was the same pickup his father had once driven, usually piled high with newly restored wooden furniture or Christmas trees for sale. And with Jens. The handsome little chap would sit in the middle of it all, bobbing along happily, his face fresh and clear.

★

His beginning was promising. Jens Horder was a much-loved child, as was his brother, Mogens, and in many ways the two boys lived a charmed life with their parents out on the Head. They were each other's best friends, the island was their playground, and as their father showed them how

17

to help him in his workshop, in due course it also became their place of work.

Their father, Silas, was a man of many talents, but above all he was a skilled carpenter. Doing his best was a matter of honour for him, he regarded every tree as precious, a wonder of nature, and treated each one with the greatest respect from the moment it shot up from the ground, regardless of whether it ended its life as firewood, planks, furniture or a desiccated Christmas tree. Or outlived him. Certain chosen trees were turned into beautifully decorated coffins and would thus return to the earth from which they had once grown.

Both boys inherited their father's talent for carpentry, but that was where the similarity between them ended.

Jens was the younger. The younger, the darker and more handsome, his mother used to think, when the boys played outside and she would watch them from the kitchen window. Mogens, however, had a much brighter mind in every way, and that reassured her. It boded well for the business when the time came for the boys to take over. Else Horder had such faith in her older son's business acumen that she was privately convinced that Mogens would one day outshine his father.

Because Silas might be a highly respected carpenter, but when it came to financial matters his talent was limited. The money came in but was soon spent on unnecessary items rather than to purchase the essentials, which should have been the main objective of his business. He was a frequent visitor to the main island's two second-hand shops, and he had a rare talent for coming across barns full of stuff that people were keen to get rid of. Silas would invariably return with some find or other he was delighted with.

His wife rarely approved, but Silas just couldn't help himself. Besides, he was adamant that he would find a use for whatever it was someday. It was all about having an eye for things, he insisted. For their potential. Great treasures could be found among the lowliest of objects. After all, hadn't he made a lovely chandelier from twelve old horseshoes? Else was forced to concede that indeed he had. It was incredibly beautiful and different. He had even sold a couple of chandeliers to tourists visiting the south coast of the main island and so been able to finance the purchase of more old horseshoes.

Silas's talent for woodwork extended beyond carpentry; he also knew how to look after wood before it came under his plane. In fact, he cared for all the trees on the Head as if he were their father. As far as his actual sons were concerned, he had shared his love and knowledge as best as he could: Jens loved the forest with all his heart and Mogens loved it with his mind. In other words, Jens would have a lump in his throat when he saw a tree being felled, while Mogens would be busy calculating its value.

Silas Horder loved his sons equally, of course. But it was possible he loved Jens a little more.

The idea of expanding the existing mixed forest with a small area of Christmas trees was the most visionary idea Silas had ever had, and certainly the most lucrative. It would enable him to supply Christmas trees and ornamental branches to the island's permanent residents and the few people who spent Christmas in their holiday cottages, and thus make money for more treats on the Horder family's Christmas table. That, however, happened only when Else Horder managed to keep hold of the money before Silas spent it on more junk.

They had plenty of room to plant Christmas trees because the family had all the Head to themselves. No one else appeared interested in living so remotely, even before trees and bushes began to spread out of control and suffocate the open areas where animals used to graze. However, the locals were happy to visit the Head in order to have something mended or simply for a chat, even though it was a long walk or drive up the narrow isthmus. The island's inhabitants respected Silas. They valued his craftsmanship and found his eccentricity amusing. It was common knowledge, for instance, that he talked to his trees, and his Christmas trees were always popular; customers especially liked to hear him whisper goodbye to the tree before selling it to them. Afterwards he would rub his hands in the December cold and look a little mournful while his wife took the money.

So Silas was no ordinary man, but no one doubted his goodness, and the coffins he made were so beautiful that it was regarded as something of a privilege to be buried in one of them.

No one apart from Silas Horder himself and his younger son knew that the coffins were tested before they were handed over to their rightful owners. On the night that followed the completion of a coffin, the pair of them would sneak out into the workshop when Else and Mogens were fast asleep. They would lie down in the coffin, Silas first, with Jens on his stomach, enveloped in the darkness and the scent of fresh wood.

Jens knew no nicer or safer feeling. Years later, when the hours in the coffins had blurred into vague childhood memories, that feeling would remain. Darkness was a trusted friend. A loving embrace.

They would chat about the bike-shop owner or the baker or whoever had just died and would soon be occupying the coffin. Silas knew most people on the main island, or he knew someone who knew them. Not that he was a gossip. He only ever spoke well of the dead. It might be something like how the baker had always been good to his rats, or how the postmaster had had such an excess of love for his wife that he had had to share his devotion with no fewer than three other women on the main island.

Silas also confided in his younger son that for years the mayor of Korsted had hidden things around his farm which they were allowed to take, but only if they could be as quiet as mice and invisible and never talk to anyone about it afterwards, including the mayor himself. It was an amusing little game, which the mayor played with a few initiated people. After his death other people on the island carried on the game, but it was a big secret, and Jens must never say a word about it to Mogens or anyone else. Especially not his mother, who didn't like that sort of game.

What was said in the coffin stayed in the coffin. That was the deal.

*

However, not everything that was put in the coffin stayed there. On the night they were testing out the baker's coffin Jens had a sudden flash of inspiration just before he climbed on to his father. He spun around and started rummaging through a box behind the lathe.

'What are you doing, Jens?' his father called out from the coffin.

'I want to put the baker's rolling pin inside,' Jens whispered proudly when he came back. 'Don't you think he'll be pleased to have it with him in the coffin, even though the handle has cracked?'

There was a small bang when one end of the rolling pin hit the bottom of the coffin. It took a while before Silas said:

'Naaaah, I'm not sure about that. After all, I've had it for some time now, Jens, and I've grown very fond of that rolling pin – otherwise, why do you think I've kept it? There's no need to bury a perfectly good item that's still in working order. And it can serve to remind us of the old baker. No, it's better that it stays here with us. The baker won't need it where he's going.'

'You mean in the coffin?' Jens whispered.

'No, I was thinking more about afterwards.'

'Afterwards? Where's he going afterwards?'

'Well, that depends on whether he has been good.'

'At baking?'

'No, I didn't mean at baking. It's more about whether he treated people properly while he was alive.'

'He once threw a piping bag at me.'

'Did he now?'

'Yes, because I stopped to touch the doorframe of the bakery. It was the frame you made for him last spring.'

'And did you take the piping bag with you?'

'Yes.'

'Good boy.'

'So where is he going?'

'Hard to know, but that's for nature to decide. When his body decomposes in the coffin, his soul will leave and turn into something else. Whatever he deserves to become.'

'What might that be? A butterfly? A blade of grass? A cart for a horse?' Jens wondered out loud. 'A fatted pig?' He could easily imagine the baker as a fatted pig.

'Who knows?'

'Might he become a baker again?'

'I hope not.'

'But he'll stay on the island?'

'Who knows?'

Jens mulled over that night's conversation in the coffin. He found it comforting to know that not everything ended when you died. But then again he didn't like not knowing what he would become. He would prefer to carry on living as himself. And he certainly didn't want to be a mosquito. He would rather be an ant; at least it didn't fly around and sting people. Or a tree that might become a fine coffin in which someone might lie and have a chat someday.

He pondered death at length, but there was one thought in particular that he wished had never occurred to him: that it wasn't just him who was going to die. His mother and Mogens would also die at some point. As would his father. And regardless of what they became afterwards, they would no longer be his mother and Mogens and his father. He had a tummy ache for several days at the realization, and it made him wonder whether it might not be better to die before them so that he wouldn't have to go around missing them. But then they might go around missing him and be sad about it. And if he became a tree or a horse or a scarecrow after his death, would they even notice? He couldn't imagine anything more awful than being a scarecrow that no one recognized and was reduced to just standing there frightening the birds. And might he become a rolling pin? What if he cracked?

The thoughts jumbled around his head, and he had the most dreadful nightmares about being taken to the junkyard. He had once visited the junkyard on the main island with his grandfather with a pile of broken things his mother refused to look at any longer. By the time they came back, Silas had returned from the forest. It was the first time the boys had seen their father angry. His face went puce when he realized they had driven off with the stuff without his permission. It took their mother most of the afternoon to appease her husband. But eventually the two of them sat holding hands on the bench while their relieved sons kicked a ball around the yard.

Sometime later their grandfather died. To begin with, Mogens and Jens thought they were meant to be sad, but they were told that there was nothing to be sad about because their grandfather was an old man who was pretty much ready to die. Nor had they known him very well because he had lived in the southern part of the island, rarely visited the Head and barely said a word even when he was there. So it wasn't as if he left a great void. Even so, Jens couldn't help wondering what his grandad had hoped to become. And whether he had succeeded.

On the night his grandfather's coffin was ready, Jens could finally get his concerns off his chest. He was lying snug and comfortable on his father's soft tummy, with his father's big, warm hands on his chest. Every now and then he could feel Silas's beard on his forehead, and though it was a little scratchy, it felt nice. They breathed in unison.

'What do you think Grandad will become?'

'He was a nice man. I think he'll become something good.'

'So not a mosquito?'

'No, I would find that hard to believe.'

'A tree?'

'Yes, a tree is more likely. A big, tall pine.'

'Then we'll have to be careful that we don't chop him down.'

Jens could tell from the movement of his beard that his father was smiling.

'It's fine to chop down a tree if you value the life it has lived. As far as your grandad is concerned, he may not always have made the right decisions, but he was a good and loving person who wouldn't say boo to a goose. We'll remember him for that.'

Jens had visited his grandad in Sønderby a couple of times. He had no idea that he had kept geese. All he knew was that his grandad had had a small dog that followed him everywhere and could play dead on command. That was fine until one day when it didn't get up. Ever since then it was known as the most obedient dog on the island, and Jens's grandad stopped saying anything. Then he, too, died.

'He wouldn't have been mean to his dog, would he? I mean, on purpose?' Jens asked anxiously.

'You're also a good person, Jens. No, your grandad never hurt a fly. And now you've inherited his cap. You can wear it even if it's still a little too big for you. That's a nice way to remember him, don't you think?'

Jens nodded in the darkness.

'Will I be someone's dad one day?' he asked out of the blue.

'Yes, I think so.'

'If I have a son, I'm going to call him Carl.'

'Carl? Why Carl?'

'The poet I chatted to down at the junkyard says his name is Carl and that he's more than a hundred years old. He says he expects to live to two hundred.'

'Is that what he says?' Silas coughed.

'Yes, if you count the rings in his face it looks about right. He has lots and lots of them.'

'I see. Well, I'll try to do that when I see him next. If I have enough time.'

'And if I have a daughter, I'll call her Liv, just like the little newborn girl we saw yesterday.'

'It's a beautiful name.' Silas smiled again.

'Yes.'

They lay for a while listening to the susurration of the trees which came in through a crack in the window. The sound was accompanied by a scent of spruce and wet moss that mixed with the aroma of the wooden coffin. Soon the honeysuckle would join in.

Silas Horder began to stir.

'Right, I think the coffin is ready for Grandad now. Time for us to go to bed. Mind you don't wake your brother when you go back.'

'I've *never* done that.'

'No, you're right. Then again, Mogens sleeps like a log.'

That night Jens didn't sleep a wink. He was thinking. What if a log was really a sleeping person who was too tired to become anything else?

The funeral went well, Else told them when she returned from Korsted church. Mogens and Jens had stayed on the Head with their father. Silas might be fond of coffins, but he hated funerals, and he didn't like the boys leaving home either. It was bad enough that they sometimes had to go to school rather than help him in the workshop, in the forest or with the animals. There were plenty of things for the two of them to do. Besides, Silas didn't have much faith in the knowledge his sons acquired at school. Sometimes he didn't understand a word of what Mogens was talking about. Whoever heard of *square* roots?

It was enough to make Jens seriously doubt their education. Thankfully, both sons had a considerable talent for carpentry, Mogens probably the more so. Jens, however, had something unique about him which Silas couldn't put into words but adored.

The first coffin initiation had come about pretty much by chance. He had only intended to let the boy experience

the thrill of being enveloped by the wood and the craftsmanship he would himself one day master to perfection.
Let him experience the lines, the proportions, the smell of
the wood. Tell him how the tree was still alive and working
around the body. Stuff his son's schoolteacher was unlikely
to bother with.

He hadn't intended for their coffin inaugurations to continue but, lying there secretively, holding his younger son
and listening to his thoughts and confidences and questions,
imbued his life with a purpose it had previously lacked.

Silas wasn't interested in anyone else's opinion on the
matter. It never even crossed his mind that the ritual might
seem a little bizarre in other people's eyes. He cared only
that this – their safe and trusted private place – should
endure for as long as possible.

Jens was careful not to breathe a word to his big brother
about the important discoveries he had made in the coffin.
One question, however, was pressing.

'Mogens, what do you want to be?'

'When I grow up? An inventor – an inventor, definitely.'

'Sure, but what about when you die? Then what do
you want to be?'

Mogens stared at him for a moment.

'But I won't. I'm not going to die. I'm going to invent
something that will keep me alive, and it's going to make
me so much money that I can make a living from it too.
But don't tell anyone. I promise to keep you alive as well.'

There was so much that Jens couldn't tell anyone.

*

One autumn night Jens and Mogens were lying awake in their room, listening to the wind tearing at the roof tiles and knocking things over. It was a long-lasting, powerful northern wind that was now culminating in a furious storm. Over in the barn, the half-door squeaked on its hinges until a sudden gust of wind made it fly open with a bang, which was followed by a strange cacophony of whinnying and mooing and braying. Shortly afterwards they heard another door slam and the sound of their father calling out to the animals. And more noises. Something falling from the roof. The weathervane? Something rolled across the gravel and bashed into something else. Mogens guessed it was one of the barrels crashing into the pump, and quickly reassured Jens that the upheaval would have been much worse had the storm come from the south or the west. When the wind came from the north, as it did tonight, the forest would bear the brunt of it for them. Besides, the trees were so far away that they wouldn't hit the house if they keeled over, so Jens had nothing to worry about.

But Jens wasn't comforted. On the contrary, he was horrified at the thought of the poor trees giving their lives to protect his home. A loud, ripping sound followed by a hollow thud from the forest made his throat tighten. He pressed himself against Mogens, who held his baby brother in a loving embrace while he fantasized about inventing an effective storm shield to the south and expanding the workshop to the west.

The next morning they walked around the house and the outbuildings with their father to inspect the damage. Nothing serious had happened to the buildings, but stuff had been scattered all over the place, and they spent some time picking it up and piling it up along the walls – pretty much where it had all stood to begin with. The animals had long since settled down and were chewing the cud in their modest quarters.

Afterwards they went into the forest to see the extent of the wind's ravaging. At first they walked through the Christmas-tree plantation, which had survived remarkably unscathed, and then along the winding paths in the mixed forest, where a few spruces lay like fallen soldiers in the mist. One or two had ripped up whole chunks of the forest floor so it looked like a thick shield of soil and roots was rising from the yawning hole. Jens walked carefully up to one of them and stared into the underworld that had opened up in front of him: roots of varying shapes and sizes sticking out from the vertical soil in every direction like exposed tentacles, a few brutally snapped, others pulled out in thin, thirsty strips. At the bottom the most stubborn roots still clung to the soil, and at the top a blanket of moss hung over the edge like a waterfall that had changed its mind halfway down. Nothing remained of the forest floor's usual natural order and quiet harmony, but even this unfamiliar chaos beckoned Jens with a shivering delight.

Soon he felt a pair of familiar hands on his shoulders.

'We'll leave it alone,' Silas whispered above him. 'I bet a fox will make its home down there. It was a very old tree. Maybe she was ready to die.'

Jens nodded. Mogens started measuring the tree.

*

The boys followed their father down the narrow forest path that wound its way through spruce and pine and oak and birch and aspen, and every time Silas ducked under a branch Jens would duck too, even though he wasn't in danger of being hit by it for a few more years. His stomach lurched when they passed the tall spruces and carried on northwards. The boys were under strict instructions to go no further than the tall spruces when they were alone in the forest, and Jens had never dared defy them. He stared, at once scared and mesmerized, at the forest of crooked pine trees that replaced the spruces. They seemed to be stretching out their branches towards him, and he couldn't decide whether it was to embrace him or strangle him. Silas would appear to pick up on his younger boy's apprehension because he stopped for a moment and put his hand on a long, twisted arm reaching halfway across the path.

'Look, Jens. I call these gnarled old pines my troll trees. They're very friendly trees that like to say hello.'

Jens nodded happily. Then he too clasped the knobbly branch and greeted the trunk politely.

The path curved and suddenly there was noticeably more space between the trees. The white mist which had lain across the forest all day had slowly drifted south. At that moment the troll trees ended completely and left the scene to the afternoon sun, which lit up the forest floor, revealing a myriad of life: glossy beetles struggling across steaming grassy mounds; insects dancing in the air between the tree trunks; a shrew's ceaseless pottering between blades of grass. A rabbit darted past them as if it wanted to catch up with the fog, and in a quivering, silvery web a

31

spider rushed towards its prey, seemingly oblivious to the cross it carried on its back.

Jens held his breath when they passed the furthest trees and stepped out into the open area that separated the forest from the sea. This was the common. The mysterious, large common he knew only from his father's and big brother's descriptions and from his own dreams at night.

'Look how the heather blossoms,' Silas said. 'And try smelling it . . .'

They heard him take a deep breath in through his nose. Jens did likewise as he looked at the purple carpet spread out in front of them. The scent was new and captivating: the fresh, salty sea air was scented with the heather and the coarse grass. Jens thought that this had to be the most peaceful spot in the whole world. He would love to lie here chatting to his father for ever and ever.

'Look at those ones over there . . . They're called devil's-bit.' Silas pointed at some round blue flowers balancing on long stems in between the heather and the grass.

'Devil's-bit?'

All Jens knew about the devil was that, according to the vicar's wife, he reigned in the postmaster's home. Judging from her tone of voice, it was a sorry state of affairs, and Jens hoped that it would soon be handed in to the workshop to be fixed, so that he could finally get to see it for himself.

'Yes, and this summer I'll show you the other flowers that grow out here. There's one called bird's-foot trefoil . . .'

Now he was talking. There were plenty of birds on the

island, according to Mogens, but Jens still wasn't altogether sure what made a girl a bird. Perhaps it had to do with being hen-pecked.

'And the Virgin Mary's bed straw . . .'

Jens's jaw dropped, and he looked at his father: 'This is where she sleeps?'

He had heard about the Virgin Mary at school and knew that she had a donkey and was married to a carpenter. He couldn't remember anything else, but it had been enough for him to warm to her immediately.

Silas smiled. 'Not as far as I'm aware, but if she did decide to lie down here, at least she'd be comfortable,' he said with a wink to Jens, who thought his father had got something in his eye.

Mogens wasn't listening. He was shifting his weight from foot to foot, eager to get to the sea. Once they were ordered to scare off any vipers that might hide in the heather, his shifting turned into enthusiastic stomping. Jens stayed between his father and his brother. The viper was the only animal apart from mosquitoes that he really hated.

'Come on, Jens, come on,' Mogens urged him as he raced down to the beach to the point where the sea had last drawn a line in the sand. He fell to his knees in his short trousers and waited. A moment later the water returned and trickled softly under his hands and knees and the tips of his shoes so that he sank slightly into it and got a little wetter than he had expected. Mogens grinned happily.

Jens stayed put in the lyme grass, which tickled his legs like tiny needle pricks over his knee-high socks, but he barely felt it. He was mesmerized by his big brother and the sea.

When the sea crept across the beach it resembled a thin, shiny tongue. But there was nothing ferocious about the tongue. It licked Mogens's knees carefully, like a loving cat would have done. Jens concluded that the sea must be nice. For some reason he had always imagined that the sea up here would be scary. Now he felt safe about everything that lay to the north.

He had often sat on the back of the pickup truck and gazed at the sea as a blue surface either side of the Neck when they rattled down the gravel road to the main island. And he had also seen it between the hills as they approached Korsted or delivered restored furniture to the islanders. It was always there, a surrounding danger and a distant sound. But he had yet to touch it. He had never taken off his shoes and socks and stepped out into it and felt it whirl softly past his ankles before it was pulled back with a small whoosh in the sand under his feet. And he had never bent down and felt it flow between his fingers – cold, soft, incomprehensible.

Until now.

While the boys played at the water's edge they noticed their father walking up and down and staring intently at a ribbon of seaweed and pebbles lying like an uneven lace border along the sloping shore where the water and the beach exchanged caresses. Silas had his hands on his back and was leaning slightly forwards as he put one foot in front of the other. At times he would stop and rummage around in the pebbles before carrying on in the same, slow pace.

'Perhaps he's prospecting for gold?' Mogens whispered.

Perhaps he's looking for Grandad? Jens wondered to himself.

Silas was scouting for amber, and he found what he was looking for. More than he could have hoped for. The boys stared curiously at the small golden-brown nugget he held up to them. He explained how they could tell that it was amber rather than a stone and let them bite it gently.

'Is it worth a lot of money? Like gold is?' Mogens wanted to know.

'Large pieces of amber can be valuable, as it's also used for jewellery-making. But no, it's not valuable in the same way as gold.'

'So what *is* it? Where does it come from?' Jens asked.

Silas smiled. 'I'll show you in a moment, but first I want you to take a look at this.' He stuffed his hand into his pocket and produced another golden nugget, this one slightly bigger.

'In one sense this is worth more than gold. Take a look at what's hiding inside it.'

'It looks like . . . an ant?' Jens whispered.

'It *is* an ant. And the special thing about this ant is that it's very, very old. People have found lumps of amber with animals several million years old in them.'

'Big animals as well?'

'No, mostly small animals, I believe. But just imagine: the amber preserves them. Amazing, isn't it?'

The boys nodded in unison, without taking their eyes off the ant. Suddenly Jens looked up at his father, wide-eyed.

'But what about people? Small people . . . children? Have they also found ancient children inside a piece of amber?'

Silas shook his head, ignoring Mogens's giggles. 'No, I've never heard of that.' Then he scratched his beard, as he always did when he remembered something interesting. 'And yet . . .'

Mogens fell silent immediately.

'A long time ago . . .' Silas began. 'No, come with me. It's better that I show you.'

Silas didn't elaborate but led his sons across the heather and back through the forest. It had grown a little cooler but the sun was still in the western sky, squeezing long rays in between the tall spruces.

'We're looking for an injured tree,' he said, finally veering off the path to wander between some pines. 'Look for one whose bark has been damaged.'

Seconds later Mogens found one. '*Over here!*' he yelled, so loudly you would think he had struck gold.

Mogens couldn't have found a better tree. Silas Horder had known all along that there was a pine with a wound at a child's eye level right there. He knew all his trees.

'Good job. Now take a close look at it. Do you see those golden drops? That's a kind of sap that exists inside the tree. When the bark is damaged, the sap runs to the cut, fills it up and thickens. It helps to heal the tree and so keep pests at bay. Try touching it . . . it's sticky . . . then sniff your fingers afterwards.'

'It smells gross,' Mogens said.

'I think it smells nice,' said Jens.

'You think it smells nice,' Silas echoed in a kind voice. Then he took out the lump of amber with the ant from his pocket. 'What you can see on the tree is called resin. And this small piece of amber here is ancient resin from an ancient tree.'

'. . . in which an ancient ant was caught?'

'Exactly.'

'So what about the children?' asked Jens, who hadn't forgotten the sentence their father had started at the water's edge.

'Well, I remembered that the ancient Egyptians – they were people who lived a very long time ago – used resin to embalm their dead.'

The boys looked at him blankly.

'The Egyptians believed that the soul continued to live in the dead body, you see, if you treated the body in such a way that it wouldn't decay. And they tried to do that using resin.'

'Are you telling me it didn't rot?' Jens had eagerly followed the decomposition of a dead fox cub on the roadside verge just below the Neck. It had turned very dark and flat over time. And swarmed with flies.

'How could they prevent that?' Mogens asked. 'What exactly did they do?'

'This is where it gets a bit technical.' Silas laughed. 'But, all right . . . first they removed internal organs such as the lungs, the liver and the intestines and so on from the body, just like you see me do when I gut an animal.'

The boys nodded eagerly.

'However, they left the heart in place; the dead person would need it. Then they cleaned the body thoroughly and dried it by putting it in a salt bath. Salt draws out all the moisture, and absolutely no moisture must remain in the body. It's moisture that causes it to rot. Once the body was dry they coated it in liquid resin and various oils and wrapped it in bandages. Including the face and toes.' Silas could not help feeling delight at the knowledge he was imparting. They were unlikely to be taught this in school.

'Bandages?' Jens said, tasting the word.

'Yes, strips of thin fabric . . . like the ones I tied around your arm when you hurt yourself. They would also paint a portrait of the dead person and place it where the face was hidden by the fabric.'

'But then what did they do with the body afterwards?' asked Mogens, his brow furrowed. He was trying to understand all the details of the process.

'They would put the body in a kind of coffin, which they left in a dry place so as to preserve it as well as possible. And it worked. Archaeologists have found embalmed bodies several thousand years old.'

'Including children?'

'Yes, I'm pretty sure they have also found embalmed children.'

Mogens looked at the small amount of resin which the tree in front of them had produced. 'But how do you get a lot of it?' he asked, scratching his chin, for want of a beard.

'You can drain it from the trees in such a way that you

get quite a lot. I might show you one day. Time to go home. Your mother will be waiting with dinner.'

'He told you *what*?'

Jens had rarely seen his mother's eyes so big and wide as when he told her about that day's adventures. His father and Mogens were seeing to the animals, and he was help-ing set the table. She didn't seem entirely happy to hear about the ancient children and the resin.

From that meal on Jens took great care to make sure that what was said in the forest stayed in the forest.

# Stricken

Things went well until they didn't. Silas Horder was found by his younger son, who dragged his dead father across the heather, through the forest and into the farmyard, where he laid him on the gravel under a blindingly bright noon sun.

Whereupon Jens himself collapsed from exhaustion next to his father.

No one could fathom how the boy had managed to drag his father that far. All right, so Jens had turned thirteen, but he was of slender build and not nearly as big and strong as his brother, who was four years older.

Despite his exhaustion, Jens refused to leave the body. He would grip his father's shirt and scream whenever anyone came near. It was hours before his big brother could lift him up and carry him inside. At that point Jens was sleeping like a log.

It was thought that Silas had been struck by lightning while out on the common, because he had burns to his leg and back, beautiful, intricate branching that looked like the work of an artist. There had indeed been a short bout of thunder that same morning, but it had passed before anyone had really noticed.

A few days later Silas was buried at Korsted cemetery in

a mass-produced coffin, witnessed by a handful of silent islanders, a deeply distraught widow and her older son.

Her younger son refused to attend.

After his father's death Jens grew very quiet. When he skived off school, something he soon did on a regular basis, he would roam around the main island and secretly explore people's outhouses and barns. He preferred to be alone in the workshop or in the forest before daybreak. Eventually he stopped showing up for school at all, and Else Horder didn't mind. He worked hard in the workshop, took good care of the animals and looked after the trees with a sense of great responsibility; deep down, that was what really mattered.

On the death of his father, Mogens assumed the main responsibility for the carpentry business. The orders kept coming in. It was well known that the sons had not only inherited their father's business but also his talent.

Not that many people were in need of a carpenter these days, though. Buying new things had become so easy, but the islanders tried to help. For that reason they were prepared to overlook the fact that Mogens had started to drive the pickup truck without it being one hundred per cent legal for him to do so. After all, he was a perfectly competent driver. And when one day it was Jens driving the pickup truck down Korsted high street, with a couple of newly fixed windows, it was simply regarded as a natural progression.

The years flowed into one another.

Else had always been able to see her husband in her younger son, but as Jens grew older the similarities became more obvious. His mouth took on the exact same shape as his father's: a wistful line, rising to a hint of a smile at the corners, like the expression on a much-loved teddy bear that was delighted with all the hugs it gets but miserable that it can't give any back. Jens had also inherited his father's gaze. His warm, almost pitch-black eyes had the same dreamy light.

Jens, however, had grown more introverted than Silas had ever been. His remoteness and chronic silence bordered on avoidance of human contact, and this worried Else. She desperately wanted him to let her into his world, make her his confidante, as his father had once been. To show her the same trust. And at the same time she was oddly frightened of what she might find in there. In the darkness. It was as if something had broken inside him, and she wasn't sure that it could be fixed.

Mogens didn't appear to have been affected by the death of his father in the same way. He seemed to put grief and the loss behind him relatively quickly and move on. He was different to Jens; that much was already clear. His approach was more rational. He had dreams, of course. But he would see those dreams through. And he possessed a sense of order, which Jens lacked. Mogens's corner of the workshop was as neat and tidy as his younger brother's was messy and disordered.

Else Horder never stopped wondering how two brothers could turn out so differently. Ever since Mogens had been a little boy, she had sensed in him an urge to achieve, grow, expand and break the mould in everything he did. He ran and jumped, preferably in the light; he was in constant motion towards new adventures.

Jens didn't jump. Nor did he break any moulds. He preferred to just be where he was, and preferably on his own. When he worked he became one with the thing he was working on; he could become so absorbed by it that he would carry on working even though it had long since grown so dark you'd have thought it would be practically impossible to do so.

Late one night Else found him sleeping soundly under the lathe on a bed of wood shavings. There was a profound innocence about Jens as he lay there in the darkness, breathing quietly. At that moment she thought that her younger son must be the gentlest person in the world.

In the time that followed Silas's death, the knowledge of Mogens's skill and sense of duty had allowed Else to hope that, together, the three of them would be able to navigate the future. However, she began to worry when, after a few years, Mogens started leaving the Head more and more often. In the end he was going off to the main island every day under some pretext or other; she could never quite fathom why. The pickup truck would usually be empty, whether he was coming or going. She began chiding him, but that only made him defiant and resulted in him staying away even more.

One day she called out to him as he was walking towards the pickup truck, before he had time to drive off. Jens heard them from the workshop, where he was hunched over a chest of drawers that needed new feet.

There was a bang as his mother slammed open the kitchen window.

'Mogens, are you off again? Without any deliveries? Why don't you lend your brother a hand in the workshop? Where are you off to this time? Is this about a girl? Why don't you stay here and make yourself useful? Jens tells me you have spruces to fell today. You're not going to let him do it all on his own? Again?'

Jens had heard it all before, more times than he could count, but today the sounds were different. Mogens's footsteps in the gravel stopped before they reached the pickup truck. Then it seemed like he had turned around.

Jens raised his head and listened out.

'Mogens?' Else called out. 'Stay right there. Who do you think you are? What do you think you're doing? What are you doing with that bicycle . . . ?'

'I'm *suffocating* here.'

Jens heard a few small hops and then the sound of a bicycle being pedalled through the gravel. The crunching turned into a distant rattling and was soon eclipsed by the singing of a lark. When Jens looked out of the window, he could see nothing but the empty pickup truck parked in the blindingly bright noon sun.

Some months later they received a letter containing some money. There was an 'M' on the back of the envelope. The next month another letter arrived, and this continued month after month. Else Horder paid her bills on time; Jens didn't say anything. Nobody asked any questions. Including the postman, who wondered privately about the widow and the younger son and the letters from 'M'.

★

Else Horder's health began to suffer. She suffered pain. In her 'rectum', as the doctor put it. At times she would bleed and she had to wear a device under her clothing, which embarrassed her. She struggled to manage the housework, something she had otherwise enjoyed and had made a point of doing diligently all her life. It upset her, and the bitterness, in turn, caused her even more pain.

There were days when she couldn't even get out of bed.

It became clear that they could no longer manage on their own, so Else decided to bring in hired help. As long as Jens continued making some money from repairs, they could afford it. The girl could live in the room that Mogens had furnished for himself in the workshop building; it even had its own entrance from the yard. It was known as 'the white room' because Mogens had insisted that it should be light.

Else never once doubted that the monthly brown envelopes from M would continue, and they did indeed arrive with a regularity which she appreciated. However, she didn't have the energy to consider whether she should feel grateful to her older son.

A pretty young woman from the mainland applied for the position. She was the only applicant, incidentally, because the local young women preferred to travel to the mainland to look for work. Many of them had also started dressing in a way that made Else uncomfortable. She especially disapproved of the many of them who chose not to wear a bra under their blouse. Else didn't regard herself as old-fashioned, and a pair of wide bell bottoms on the Head wouldn't upset her, but she drew the line at the lack of a bra. There had to be limits to frivolity.

Maria Svendsen was a gift from heaven: she wore a modest bra and sensible trousers.

★

Maria normally wore her hair up so it wouldn't get in the way, but when she didn't her long blonde hair settled in small, soft waves around her face and neck. Jens happened to see it one day when he glanced through the window of the white room. He quickly looked away but was unable to forget the image of Maria with her hair down, smiling at him through the window.

Every now and then she would visit him in the workshop and they would chat about the weather and the furniture. She skilfully avoided speaking out of turn about his mother, but even so Jens soon surmised that Else was hard to please.

To begin with, however, they hardly spoke because Maria was by nature almost as monosyllabic as Jens had become over time. But in their mutual taciturnity Maria gradually found the courage and confidence to speak up. She started talking about her household chores and the tasks she had yet to do that day, and Jens listened to every single little detail with interest and gratitude.

Soon her stories extended beyond the Head, even beyond the island. She talked about her childhood on the mainland, about her hard-working parents. About school, which she hadn't liked because everyone was so horrible – and yet she loved reading and writing more than anything on earth.

Then she talked about the books she had read, and

the books she wanted to read. And she told him how she would copy pages purely for the pleasure of writing, and sometimes extend the passages she had copied just to write creatively. And how she would write down her thoughts, simply to get them out of her head. And how she would press her nose against the paper in order to smell it.

And when she had her nose pressed against the paper, Jens found something to contribute. 'Did you know that paper is made from wood?' he asked.

Jens's fascination with Maria grew with every day. There was a lightness about her that he had never experienced with any other human being. Possibly because he hadn't met many people from the mainland. Perhaps they were all lighter over there.

He listened to her bright voice, which said so little and yet so much. When she finally did start to speak, it was completely effortless. And when she breathed, she did it so calmly and so deeply you'd think she was conscious of it each time.

She wasn't, but Jens was pretty much aware of every single breath Maria inhaled through her small nostrils and deep into her soft body. And although he didn't dare look at her directly, he would still see her chest heave under her blouse, and hear the sound that accompanied it, and he was reminded of the waves rolling calmly on to the northern shore when you went there late in the afternoon with your father and your big brother. The quiet whoosh, the quiet swell and then the quiet whoosh again. A reassuring continuity.

Yes, that was exactly how it sounded when Maria breathed. At times it would make Jens forget to breathe.

And her mouth was wondrous.

It was as if a smile that could never be driven out by melancholy lived in the soft corners of her mouth. He was convinced that, even when Maria cried, she would still smile a little, in the same way that a horse always hides an inscrutable smile in its dark muzzle.

Jens sensed strength in her softness, a foundation of serenity behind her caution, but also gentleness in her inexplicable strength, which she demonstrated when she went about her chores. He saw her lug around basins and laundry and bedlinen and firewood and pots and sacks without ever stopping to wipe the sweat from her brow. And he saw her tend to the animals as if she had never done anything else. Without fear and without hesitation, with soft, strong hands and a voice they understood. The animals loved her.

Jens was with them in that.


He showed her the forest in September, and she laughed when he got resin in his hair. He showed her the sea in March, and she laughed when his socks got wet. He showed her the common in June, and she kissed him on the Virgin Mary's bed straw.

*Dear Liv*

*There are choices I should not have made. Perhaps I should never have met your father. Perhaps things would have been much simpler if I had stayed on the mainland and married my politician cousin, as my father begged me to. It would have ensured that the business would continue, he said. And I did love my father's bookshop.*

*But I was young, far too young. And my cousin had the most revolting, intrusive eyes, and hands that were big and coarse, although all they ever did was write speeches or issue invoices. I was scared of him and his big hands, despite my father's assurance that he was a good match – and that his party was a good party, which would look after small-business owners. Especially if you were related to him.*

*Yes, my cousin was a good match, and he was very keen on the bookseller's shy daughter. He was a lovesick and enterprising man who stood to inherit an egg-box factory from his invalid father. I think his hands would have crushed any eggs they had gripped. And I felt just as fragile as a newly laid egg then. In those days I was just as slim as you are now, believe it or not.*

*I obviously shouldn't have to do anything I didn't want to do, my father said. But I could tell from his eyes that he couldn't accept a no, and I could tell from my mother's eyes that she couldn't bear to see me in the hands of the egg-box manufacturer.*

*No matter how I chose, one of them would be broken.*

*I chose to spare my mother. And myself. Or I tried to. The year after I left, I heard that she had died from pneumonia. But at least I didn't break her heart.*

*I have since read that the egg-box manufacturer went bankrupt but that the bookshop is still there. Long ago, when I had the chance to make a telephone call, I rang the mainland to find out. I didn't say anything when my father picked up. He sounded old, but he did say, 'Svendsen's Bookshop.'*

*I like the thought that the books beat the egg boxes in the end.*

*So anyway, I travelled for a while, working as a shop assistant here and there, but I didn't really enjoy it. One day someone suggested that I look for work on the island. Down by the ferry I learned that Else Horder and her son Jens were looking for help on the Head.*

*And that's how I ended up here. With your father and your granny.*

*I'm happy to tell you, Liv, that your father was the most handsome young man I'd ever seen. And he was so gentle – with soft, tender hands and warm, dark eyes. There was nothing of my cousin about him. I felt so safe with him, and I didn't doubt for a second that this was where I wanted to be.*

*Oh, I don't know if I should tell you this – you're just a child. But I so want to tell someone. I so want to tell you.*

*The first time your father and I made love was out on the common on a sea of yellow flowers. We were both terrified of vipers, and yet we lay down there. Can you imagine? He told me about the butterflies, I remember. And the lark. And the bees. And the birds . . . it was very important that we lay among the yellow flowers; it was nature's bed for me, he said. It's the only time I've ever heard him stammer, and the only time I've seen his hand shake. And it wasn't because of the vipers. It was because of what we were about to do.*

*I can still remember how tenderly his lips met mine. He was quivering like a butterfly, and I felt like a fine and delicate flower gently unfurling. At times I still feel like that inside, fine and delicate.*

*No, I don't regret meeting your father. I fell deeply in love with him, and I still am in love with him. Somehow that makes it all worthwhile. Even as I lie here today, big and heavy. Even the business with your granny. And Carl. And all the mess. The dirt that I pretend I can't see. Everything.*

*It's all too much to take, but this is the only place I want to be. Here, with you and your father. He's a good man, Liv. I know you know that. But I want to make sure you remember it.*

*I don't know how it's going to end. After all, I only know what you tell me, and I have a feeling that you don't tell me everything. That things are going wrong. I have a hunch that things happen outside this bedroom which I mustn't be told about. Things should never have been allowed to get to this point. And yet I can't regret my love for him.*

*Perhaps he's not sick at all. Perhaps it's me. Perhaps I'm sick, because I don't regret anything.*

*Sometimes I think of your father as a butterfly trying to fly in the face of time and so he's now pupating. But perhaps so am I.*

*All my love,*
*Mum*

# Happiness

To begin with, Else Horder and the young woman felt a lot of sympathy for one another. Maria was welcomed warmly with tea and home-baked cakes, and Mrs Horder gave the impression that the two of them would get along just fine. Maria had no doubt that the widow was an honest woman, and she had never felt luckier than when she moved into the white room with the family on the Head.

The room was simple and nice, with pale curtains and white-painted wooden walls. Maria was pleased that there was no hessian on the walls or pop-star posters on the ceiling, as there had been in the last attic room she had been put up in, when she was working behind the till at a bakery. In just a few days she had got fed up with staring up at the long-haired men on the posters, not to mention the bizarre smell that lingered in the attic room. It was very different from the smells of the bakery, and even more remote from the bookshop of her childhood. She wasn't into hessian and beat music, and perhaps that explained why she had been attracted to life on the island.

Here someone had put a vase of autumn flowers on the desk and the bedlinen had such a wonderful scent of fresh air and spruce that she fell into a most pleasant sleep after her first day of work.

She even enjoyed the furniture. All of it was made by

the old carpenter, Else Horder had told her, and Maria was genuinely impressed. Everything was neatly measured and planed and sanded, and the drawer in the small desk opened without resistance when she gently pulled it out. It was empty, and she put her pens and notebooks inside it before unpacking the rest of her luggage. She lacked for nothing in the white room, except for a bookcase for her many books, which she stacked carefully against the wall. She found space under her bed for her sewing box and rolls of fabric.

Nevertheless, Maria couldn't help noticing that neatness wasn't a dominant feature of the small farm. The farmhouse – with the kitchen, pantry, hallway, bathroom and big living room, as well as the master bedroom and two smaller rooms on the first floor – wasn't exactly messy, but there were lots of things to keep track of and, not least, clean. It was obvious that Else Horder could no longer manage the task herself.

However, the barn, the workshop and the outdoor areas were in a far worse state. Things were lying about everywhere, everything from timber and furniture and old engine parts to sinks and tractor tyres and the components of a horse cart. Most of it looked as if it had been lying there for a long time and was unlikely to be of any possible use.

She had occasionally seen such places from a distance, houses surrounded by junk, and every time she had wondered: who could cope, living in a place like that?

Maria didn't dare ask Mrs Horder why the family hadn't got rid of these things long ago. It was a simple matter of loading it on to the pickup truck and making a few trips to the junkyard. All right, several trips. Seeing the mess bothered her because, now that she was part of the household, she felt a degree of responsibility for the place, not least towards the customers who would visit the workshop from time to time.

On the other hand, the workshop was exclusively Jens's domain, and that was messier than anywhere else, so perhaps there was no point trying to clear anything up. In time Maria came to see that it was primarily Jens who couldn't let go of the junk. His mother had long since given up the battle.

So, in that respect, Else Horder and Maria Svendsen were quite similar. Because Maria might also like neatness, but soon she liked Jens even more.

She was strangely drawn to him from their first meeting. They greeted one another only briefly, but she recognized his introversion and immediately felt a kind of kinship with him. A spontaneous empathy. His eyes were so dark she thought they must be black. Or was it the pupils filling them out? His hair and moustache were dark brown, his skin fine and smooth, his body slim and strong. She wanted to make him a shirt and imagined how it would fall over his shoulders and chest. Perhaps she might ask him if she could one day. Then she would have to take his measurements.

On her fifth day with them she ventured into the workshop while Else Horder was resting. The widow had told her that she was in great pain, but not where, and judging by her loud snoring, it wouldn't appear to be something that interfered with her sleep. Maria was obviously concerned that Jens's mother suffered such unbearable pain, yet she was already starting to find Mrs Horder's illness somewhat baffling.

Maria had brought Jens a pot of coffee and a slice of freshly baked cake in the hope that it would be welcome. She feared being regarded as intrusive more than anything else. The door was ajar and, as she didn't have a free hand with which to knock, she carefully pushed it open with her shoulder. He was standing by the lathe, completely absorbed in his work, and didn't notice her. She stopped for a moment and watched him. Studied his hands. They looked more like the hands of an artist than a carpenter as he ran them over the chair leg he was turning.

The floor below him was littered with sawdust and wood shavings that looked like the curling leaves of a corkscrew willow.

Maria cleared her throat. And then she cleared it again. At long last he looked up, with a rather startled expression. She immediately regretted disturbing him. But then he smiled and beckoned her closer, and next thing he ran to the kitchen for an extra cup. She could hear his footsteps on the gravel as they jogged there and back, and her heart beat a little faster. She stood still with the tray while he pushed some stuff aside and pulled out a crate to serve as a table. Then he found another stool behind some sacks in a corner and wiped it with his sleeve. Soon they were sitting alone but comfortably amid the aroma of coffee and fresh pinewood, looking bashfully at one another as their pupils widened.

The months which followed were the happiest in Maria's life. Jens's mother didn't notice anything, and they told her nothing until the day she happened to be in the barn and saw them behind the heifer, kissing.

★

Else Horder wasn't best pleased. She told the two young people that their interest in one another would undoubtedly affect their work adversely. And she told herself that it was far too soon for her younger son to find himself a girl, although other people might think it was about time.

Maria and Jens didn't agree with her, and Mrs Horder saw — to her dismay — that her feelings only caused Maria to work harder around the house. She left nothing for Mrs Horder to criticize. The same went for Jens. He worked all day in order to have time to hold Maria's hand at night. They would disappear into the white room as soon as they had drunk coffee with Else in the living room after dinner and, as time passed, the cups grew smaller and smaller.

The more she saw them lose themselves in one another, the more Else's pain increased.

She told herself that she meant well and that it was in everyone's best interests that she started dropping small amounts of dirt on to the floor which Maria had just swept, or staining the tablecloth which Maria had just washed, and turning up her nose at the food which Maria had just cooked.

'Jens, I think we had better find another helper. Maria has grown slovenly,' she confided in her son one day when Maria had business on the main island. 'I've already spoken to Mrs Angel. She's a widow, very keen and very experienced.'

Mrs Angel was also obese and looked nothing like an angel. Else thought it highly unlikely that she would ever run off with her son.

Jens's fists slammed against the table so hard that his mother's illness temporarily worsened.

'Hell, no. If Maria leaves, so do I,' he thundered. Not like a child, but like the young man Maria had made him. His voice was deeper than ever.

Else was speechless while she tried to shake off the shock. The words cut her to the heart. Jens had been defiant before, especially when he lost his father – and surely that had been understandable – but he had never gone against his mother as he did now. She was horrified that he would speak like this to the woman who loved him more than anyone in the whole world; in that respect, he very much reminded her of her other son. But above all it confirmed Else's fear that Maria had driven a wedge between her and her boy.

At that moment she heard bicycle tyres crunch against gravel. Maria was back.

'Very well, if you feel that strongly about it . . .' she said in her sweetest voice. 'You know I only want what's best for you, Jens. After all, we love each other so much, you and I. You would never abandon your sick mother, would you?'

Jens turned on his heel and left his sick mother in the living room. Else sat staring into the air and concluded that this must be one of the worst days of her life.

However, he soon returned to the living room, and

Else Horder's heart softened at the sight of her younger son, who came back with his gentle gaze and tender nature. He was smiling in the endearing way in which only her Jens could smile. His dark eyes were shining.

'Maria is pregnant.' He beamed as he said it.

They were married, in love and in haste, by the mayor of Korsted. A handful of acquaintances were witnesses and congratulated the couple while secretly wondering if a new little Horder was on the way. The bride's stomach looked a little round, didn't it? Out of common courtesy people preferred to gossip rather than ask the couple outright. Besides, everyone was delighted for them, because there was no doubt that Jens Horder had been through some tough times, first with his father dying, then with his brother's sudden disappearance, although he had never let on. Jens was a man of few words. He was friendly and helpful, as his father had been before him, but he never said more than the bare minimum. It made it practically impossible to have a normal conversation with him. In fact, few people had believed that he would ever find himself a girl, but then again, perhaps it was she who had found him. They considered the options. The girl was sweet and pretty, but also rather subdued. Was it ultimately his mother who had set it all up?

After the ceremony there were sandwiches at the pub. People toasted the happy couple and sang a traditional wedding song. One hour later Jens and Maria walked home with the groom's mother when she decided that it was time for them to leave. She was in pain.

Maria continued to sleep in the white room next to the workshop, where Jens now kept his pregnant wife company in the single bed, while his mother and her pain shared the double bed in the main house.

★

In his heart of hearts, Jens wanted a boy. In her heart of hearts, Maria wanted a girl. And Else Horder, in her heart of hearts, wanted disaster to strike.

All three of them got their wish.

Maria had twins: a boy and a girl.

Jens named the babies Carl and Liv.

It wasn't until after the children were born that Jens finally managed to get his mother to vacate the master bedroom. Moving Else into Jens's old bedroom further down the passage proved something of a battle. It was rather small and she didn't like the air in there, but as only the master bedroom was big enough for two adults and two cradles, she ran out of arguments.

No one mentioned that Maria had gained quite a lot of weight during her pregnancy. She appeared unable to shift the extra kilos, which made the single bed in the white room that they had shared until then feel increasingly small.

Jens had worked on the cradles in the months leading up to the birth, once it became clear that two children were on their way. He had never built a cradle before, and yet he was sure they were the most beautiful cradles in living memory. He had devoted loving attention to every detail, just like his father used to with the coffins. When the second cradle was finished Jens put his face inside it, closed his eyes and thought about the wonderful new life that would grow out of that little space.

His mother had been hard to please during Maria's pregnancy. It was tempting to think that it was Else's hormones – rather than Maria's – that were raging when she screamed and shouted for a sandwich or freshly washed tea towels. Sadly, the situation only deteriorated once the babies arrived. Else spent most of her time in her new bedroom, despite its smallness, and she asked to have her meals brought up there, while complaining loudly about the menu.

And although Jens also found his mother deeply irritating, he was ultimately so grateful for his wife's love and the two children he and his sweetheart had brought into the world that nothing could bring him down. And despite Else's best attempts, his attention was first and foremost directed at the twins, at Maria and at the incomprehensible joy which overwhelmed him daily.

Or at least it did for a time.

One day while Maria was in the barn and Else Horder was fast asleep in her room, Jens went to check on the children. The girl was sleeping soundly. The boy was lying on the floor below his cradle. In a pool of blood.

# My Granny

They never told me exactly what happened to my brother. All they said was that he had an accident when we were very young, and afterwards my granny went to live with her cousin on the mainland. The rest of us stayed and grew bigger. Especially Mum.

I didn't learn about the business with my granny until later. And then I learned it from her. Until then I had no idea I even had a granny. But one day she turned up out of the blue and moved into the room behind the workshop and made pancakes every morning for almost a whole month. That was December.

Dad didn't want to talk about her. He didn't even seem to want to talk *to* her, and I found it all very strange. And though her pancakes were yummy and I liked hearing her stories about the mainland, I was a bit sad at how she made Dad feel. Mum didn't like her very much either.

And it wasn't just because she snored. And I'm telling you, she could really snore. When she had her lunchtime nap, you could hear it all the way over in the main house.

We'd been just fine until then. It wasn't until my granny arrived that things went really wrong. I think something snapped in Dad. Especially when she said that she was going to take me with her to the mainland and send me to school over there. They didn't know I was standing right outside the door and heard everything.

*Dear Liv*

*Your granny took up a lot of room. Not in the same way I do; in a different way. She left when you were very little. It was a huge relief, and I hadn't expected her ever to come back after all this time. I think you were coming up for your seventh birthday.*

*I had almost managed to forget about her.*

*When I saw her again it felt like someone was gripping my throat; as if all the air had been sucked out of my lungs. Deep down, I guess, I'd hoped she had died. Now suddenly she was standing there, smiling, looking healthier and stronger than ever.*

*I didn't know what she wanted. I didn't know if she even realized what she had done to Carl, to this family. Maybe it was her medication. She had sent some letters to your dad, but every time he burned them without reading them.*

*We hadn't spoken about her since she left. Never spoken about what had happened. We had protected ourselves.*

*And her timing could not have been worse. I was pregnant again.*

*All my love,*
*Mum*

# The Return

Else Horder had understood everything immediately and felt deeply hurt when her son asked her to leave the Head.

Ordered her.

In her rage, she had initially felt that she should throw them out of the house – that it was her son who should leave. But on reflection she couldn't make herself do it. Besides, she couldn't bear the thought of living there all alone, without Silas, without Mogens, without Jens . . . with all those memories and all that pain, in almost total isolation. Her cousin on the mainland had recently been widowed and offered Else a room. Suddenly the thought of getting away from the island seemed attractive. Her way out would prove to be her salvation.

Else found it bizarre that she could have lived in the middle of God's green earth – surrounded by forest and meadows and oceans of clean air – and yet feel as trapped as she had done recently, that she could only feel as free as a bird amidst the city's intrusive facades, sharp corners and clouds of exhaust fumes. But it turned out to be so. In the city, she could breathe again. Even her illness changed character. The pain started to recede, the bleeding stopped, and in time she began to regard herself as being in good health.

Her cousin was a wise woman with a nursing background, and Else felt in safe hands in every possible respect. It was a relief for her to talk to an 'outsider'. And then there was the accommodation. Else was thrilled to be moving into a neat and tidy home. As time went by, she found it increasingly baffling how both her late husband and her younger son could live in the mess they had created around them.

Else had, she now admitted, suffered terribly since her husband's accident. Ever since he had left her without warning she had clung to the sons he had given her, but they too, it seemed, were intent on leaving her. Once Jens and Maria became parents, she had been so tormented by pain and melancholy and inexplicable rage that she couldn't stand her own company. She had deluged her daughter-in-law with unreasonable demands rather than help the new mother, and she had obstructed and scowled and snarled until she could no longer bear it.

Eventually, she had sought refuge from everything. In bed she didn't have to deal with all the horrible feelings that took control of her when she saw how happy the young couple were. She had never felt so lonely and so surplus to requirements as when the twins arrived. And she had never hated her maternal jealousy so much. It was like a straitjacket she had put on herself and didn't have the ability to wriggle out of. Her desire for forgiveness and love was mixed with an obsessive need to suffer the disgust she knew perfectly well that she deserved.

When they exiled her to the small bedroom where the walls came at her from all sides and, especially, the baby boy's daily crying corroded the mortar like acid, she had drugged herself with medication and sleep in an attempt to keep her nightmares at bay. She yearned to meet her beloved Silas in the Hereafter and find peace again.

On the day of the accident she had even prayed to die quietly in her sleep. This, too, she had confided in her cousin, who had wryly remarked that sleeping quietly had never really been Else's style.

However, there was one thing that Else never told anyone. She harboured a dreadful suspicion about the accident which she couldn't shake off:

Maria had desperately wanted a girl. Else had read so in a notebook she found at the bottom of a drawer in her bedside table. 'Thoughts', it said on the cover. Now Else knew, of course, that she shouldn't read something that was so private, but the urge to penetrate the closed world of the young couple ultimately overcame her moral scruples.

Maria had wanted a girl and her wish had come true. It was another entry in the notebook which worried Else:

*I'm so happy and grateful to have given birth to two healthy children. They're a gift. And yet I'm eaten up by frustration. The responsibility for TWO lives feels completely overwhelming, though we're two to share it. Jens is wonderful, and I love him more than life itself. But he's also, well, Jens . . . At times he disappears into himself. And God knows his mother is no help.*

*Will we manage? Will I? The boy is a bad sleeper. He cries a lot. It keeps me awake and drives me crazy. In my darkest moments I wish we had only had the girl.*

Else couldn't make herself articulate her suspicion to herself or to her cousin. And yet it tormented her increasingly as time went on.

It would be more than six years before she returned to the Head. During all that time she didn't hear a word from them. They never replied to her letters and, as they had yet to have a telephone installed, she was forced to ring the pub in Korsted, where it seemed they no longer went. One day when Else called, the landlord told her that Jens Horder was rarely in town these days. Else was genuinely worried, and the sight she encountered on the Head when she got out of the taxi did nothing to assuage her fears.

It was as if they had given up completely. The mess around the buildings was worse than ever. And it wasn't the only thing that was taking up space.

When Maria came outside to see who the unexpected visitor was Else barely recognized her daughter-in-law.

Maria's once so attractive figure had grown shapeless and she seemed horribly burdened by it. She had to support herself against the wall to walk down the two steps leading to the yard from the front door, and her light gait had been replaced by an ugly waddling.

Else tried to hide her shock.

'Hello, Maria,' she said in a friendly voice. 'It's been a long time.'

Maria nodded and proffered a strained smile. Else couldn't decide whether it was in response to the sight of her mother-in-law or her own physical challenges.

'Good afternoon, Else. What a . . . surprise. I didn't know . . . Let me get Jens.' The taxi which had brought Else from the ferry to the Head turned around slowly and disappeared down the gravel road towards the Neck and the main island. Maria looked after it briefly. 'We don't get many visitors these days,' she said.

'But surely the postman calls?' Else said, not knowing which response she would prefer.

'Yes, every now and then,' Maria said, without looking at her. 'We still get the . . . well, you know. I'll just go and get Jens.'

Else thought about Mogens. She had heard nothing from her older son for years, but she was delighted to hear that he still sent money to the Head. It had only ever said 'Horder, the Head' on the envelope, and that could be any Horder at the Head, mother as well as brother.

She herself had written 'Jens Horder' on all of hers.

The door to the workshop closed behind Maria and the steady hammering which had sounded from inside stopped abruptly.

Else's gaze followed a solitary snowflake that floated through the air until it hit the ground and disappeared. It was clear that no fresh gravel had been strewn across the farmyard for years, and most of the shingle was hidden by soil now. Grass and broken straw stuck up in many places, evidence that the yard must be rather overgrown in the summer. She looked around at the piles of junk which were steadily filling the space between the buildings and she shuddered in the cool air. A black cat emerged between some spare engine parts. When it spotted Else it slunk away immediately.

73

Shortly afterwards Jens appeared.

Else hadn't seen her son since he drove her to the ferry on the terrible day when she was exiled from her own home. Back then she had wondered whether he would in fact drop her off at the ferry or, at the last minute, at the junkyard, which wasn't far from the port. In which case it would have been the first time in years that he had dropped something off at the junkyard instead of bringing something back.

He hadn't gained weight like his wife, quite the opposite, but his beard had grown considerably. The small moustache had turned into a dense, dark full beard and his hair reached below his ears. He wore his cap, as always. Else felt strangely conflicted at the sight of Jens, who now looked more like his father rather than the child she remembered.

'Good afternoon, Mum,' he said, and gave her an awkward kiss on her cheek. She wanted to embrace him, but he quickly stepped back. 'We weren't expecting you,' he said, looking at the two big cases she had set down.

Else didn't have the energy to wonder whether he was lying or if he genuinely hadn't read the last two letters she had sent.

'I'll go back again,' she said. 'But I hope that I·may be allowed to stay here for a little while . . .' She hesitated for a moment. 'I wanted to see how you were doing.'

'We're fine,' Jens said without hesitation. 'And how are things with . . . ?'

'Cousin Karen. I really enjoy living with her, thank you. To my surprise, I like the city.'

'It can be very nice . . . the city . . . especially in December,' Maria said, which Else interpreted as an invitation to return to the delights of the city at her earliest convenience.

'How long were you intending to stay?' Jens's gaze slipped momentarily to the far end of the workshop, where the door to the white room was. Parts of a slurry spreader were lying outside it.

His mother shrugged. 'Well, I was thinking that it depends . . .'

At that moment what it depended on came running from behind the barn. She had been out in the field.

'Dad, is the ram allowed . . .?' On seeing Else, the girl stopped in her tracks. 'Who's that?' she asked, and pointed at her granny with a mixture of suspicion and curiosity. Mostly suspicion.

Else was about to reply but was intercepted by her son. 'That's a lady who'll be staying with us for a while. What about the ram?'

The girl's eyes widened. She was clearly not used to guests staying over.

'What about the ram, Liv?'

'He's knocked over one of the . . . But where's she going to stay, Dad?' Liv couldn't take her eyes off the lady who would be staying with them for a while. Else studied her granddaughter with a lump in her throat.

The child would appear to be healthy, thank God. She took after her father more than her mother. There wasn't a single gram of excess fat on her body, her hair was cut short, her eyes were dark and intense. Most people would probably take her for a boy because there was nothing girlish about her movements or clothing. She looked like she lived in a pair of worn jeans that didn't appear to have been washed for a long time. Her plimsolls had probably been white once but had clearly never been whitened, and her blouse was pretty much in tatters. She carried a knife in a leather sheath which dangled from her belt as if it were the most natural thing in the world, and judging by the condition of the wooden handle, it saw frequent use.

'The lady will stay in the white room. I'll just carry her cases over there, then I'll be back and come and check on the ram. You can move the horse round the back, if you want to.'

Liv turned around and disappeared with a happy gallop while Jens picked up his mother's luggage and marched purposefully towards the furthest end of the wooden building.

Else stared after him.

'I'll make us some coffee,' she heard behind her. And Maria walked with heavy footsteps back inside the house.

Else's fear that chaos would also reign indoors proved correct.

She struggled to find space for her cases in the white room, where there was very little white to be seen, now that things were piled up along the walls. Silas's beautiful bedroom furniture was hidden behind half-finished projects from the workshop and what looked like rubbish from the junkyard. Here was everything, from tins and chandeliers to skis and pillows and old picture frames. Everything was in a wretched condition. She couldn't imagine what use they might ever make of any of it.

Else had considered asking for her old room on the first floor, but when she saw it she dropped the idea immediately. She preferred the white room's forest of objects to the startled-looking elk head staring at her from the foot of the bed in which she had once slept.

# Light and Air

I let the horse into the pen. Usually, I'd have spent many happy hours brushing it and fussing over it with Carl, but on that day all I could do was sit down and stare at it while it wandered about, pawing the ground a short distance from me. All I could think about was the lady. No one had ever just turned up and moved in before. People from the main island came by to get things fixed, but that happened less and less, and they always drove off straightaway. And anyway, Dad said he preferred to pick up and return their stuff himself. He didn't trust them.

I didn't trust them either. I trusted my dad.

He had also started driving the Christmas trees to a yard outside Korsted to sell them there rather than have people come to us.

The lady who had turned up out of nowhere was a proper old lady with a small handbag over her arm and a coat with shiny buttons, and white hair. We had only ever seen ladies like that down on the main island. Carl was always a bit scared of them if their hair was too white, but he only ever said so to me. I'd tell him it was nothing to worry about and repeat what Dad had said: 'White hair is completely natural. We'll all have it one day. Unless we die before we get old.'

Carl and I kept a close eye on each other's hair, not to mention Dad's and Mum's. When the lady who turned out to be Granny arrived, we had yet to find a single white hair on the Head – except for the animals, of course, and the man who arrived on a three-wheel scooter to ask Dad to make an urn for his wife and a pipe for himself.

I think white hair might be a bit like grass. That once it takes root, it spreads. We certainly noticed that Dad got white hairs once Granny had moved in. Not over a few days, but overnight. When he came into the kitchen the morning after I heard them talk about me, he had plenty of white hairs in between the dark ones. Even in his beard. Carl was startled by it.

This was just before Christmas.

Before Granny arrived, I'd had the best autumn ever. Dad took me fishing for flounder. It was the first time I was allowed to come with him, and I was bursting with excitement at going fishing, but perhaps even more excited about being all alone with Dad in the dinghy. We talked about everything out there. He told me that fish didn't drown in the water but that they choked when they came up into the air.

That sounded topsy-turvy to me.

He also told me that we helped the fish by killing them before the air choked them. And when we caught a fine, flat flounder with two eyes in completely the wrong place he showed me how. He hit it over the head with a club he'd brought along specially. At first I thought it was one of the most awful things I had ever seen.

'There, Liv. It's dead now,' he said when he had whacked it. Only it couldn't be, because it was still flopping about.

I was horrified. I pointed at the fish and opened my mouth, but I couldn't get a word out.

'It's only its nerves that causes it to flop,' Dad said. 'It's completely normal. It really is dead, and I promise you that it feels nothing. We've done the best we could for that fish, so we can eat it with a clear conscience tonight.'

'But, Dad . . .'

'Yes?'

'Will the flounder come back?'

'Come back?'

'Yes, like the leaves . . . and the grass and the butterflies and the fox and the baker. You always taught me that everything comes back.'

Dad gazed across the water. He had his pipe in his mouth, and there was a wonderful aroma of smoke and sea in the dinghy. 'Yes,' he said solemnly. 'The flounder also comes back.'

I crawled closer to him and crouched down in the bottom of the dinghy to sit between his feet and smell the tar and hear the wood creak around me. Over the gunwale I could see a blue sky with fluffy clouds that didn't stir. I couldn't see the sea, but I could sense it just on the other side of the squeaking boards.

'As another flounder?' I wanted to know.

'Perhaps. Or something else, maybe.'

'Something else? A plaice?'

'Yes, why not.'

'Or a rabbit? Or . . . what about a human being?' I looked over my shoulder and tried to catch Dad's eye somewhere over his beard, but all I could see was a lot of beard and the bowl of his pipe. Maybe he shrugged, I'm not sure, but he certainly said something very strange.

'Liv, one day someone might tell you about God.'

'God? Is that the one that looks like a weever?'

'No, it's not a fish. It's . . . how can I put it? Lots of people believe in this man who is said to live in the sky and decide everything.'

'In the sky?' My eyes shifted instantly from his beard to the clouds. 'What does he look like?' I asked, and squinted.

'Oh, I don't know. They say he has a long white beard.'

Now that would really worry Carl.

'A long white beard . . . and he lives in the sky?' I said, puzzled.

'Yes, it's quite tricky to explain. But what I'm trying to tell you is that I'm not sure that they're right. I don't believe in God.'

'Because he lies?' Even then I knew with absolute certainty that lying was wrong, unless it was necessary.

'No, I mean that I don't believe he's even there.'

'Well, I've *never* seen anyone up there, so I don't believe it either,' I declared firmly. 'But I believe in that seagull.'

The beard tilted upwards for a moment, only to tip down so that I could see Dad's eyes. 'That's right. We believe in the seagull.'

I smiled. Then I slipped my dagger out of its leather sheath and held it up so the sunlight bounced off it. There was a groove in it, which I liked looking at. We had found it in the bicycle seller's outhouse, along with some other things we needed. Like tyres. And a torch and a broken parasol and a bag of liquorice.

We sat for a while, waiting.

'Mum doesn't believe in that man either, does she?'

I didn't have time to get an answer because there was another bite on the line, and we got busy landing our second flounder. This time I was allowed to help it die, and I was very good at it, Dad said. When we had caught a few more, he put away the fishing rod – and I was really disappointed.

'You should never take more from nature than you need,' he explained. 'If we catch all the fish, there won't be any left for next time.'

I understood, and looked at what we had taken. 'One, two, three . . . four flounders.'

One for each of us.

Dad smiled. Then he showed me the hook at the end of the fishing line. A long weight and some coloured beads were attached to it. 'Look at this, Liv. Tomorrow I'll show you how to make one of these weights in the workshop. I'm sure you'll be able to do it.'

And I could. And not long afterwards, I also knew how to make my very own club to whack the flounders on their heads so they died right away.

That day in the dinghy is the brightest day I can recall. Later, when I had to sit in the dark corner of the container and be very quiet, I looked back on it sometimes. It was nice to think about bright things in the dark.

It wasn't long afterwards that Dad let me come with him to set rabbit snares. It was easy to find the rabbit paths on the outskirts of the forest. Dad showed me how to place a small spruce tree across one of them and cut the branches off the tree right where the rabbits pass, making a gateway. Then we made a noose from metal wire and let it dangle from the trunk. When we checked the snare the next morning we found a dead rabbit which had jumped right into the noose. The wire was so tight around its neck you couldn't even see it for all the fur.

That night Mum made rabbit ragout with cream from the cow and thyme from the common and greens from our vegetable garden. Why spend money in the shops when we have everything we need right here? Dad would always say. He preferred to spend money only on essentials such as feed for the animals. We drove down to Vesterby for that, and most times we managed to bring home a little more than we had paid for. Dad said it was all right. They had so much down in Vesterby, and we were so nice to our animals. It was the same with the grocer's stock room. There was so much in it and so it didn't matter that I sneaked inside and helped myself to a few tins while Dad kept the grocer talking about the weather.

Later, I learned to skin and cut up the meat. Rabbits turned out to be really skinny once you remove their fur. However, the most incredible thing was looking at everything hidden inside: the pink lungs and the purple kidneys and the other bits. And the long, crinkly intestines. It crossed my mind that Mum must have a lot of that sort of thing inside her.

That autumn I also started going stag hunting on the main island. Dad knew a place near a big farm where you could often find a stag in the dark, either in the forest or out on the fields. Dad didn't like putting gunpowder into animals, and I had no idea what gunpowder was, but I decided I wouldn't like to put it inside them either. He said it was too destructive, it made an unnecessary amount of noise and that it was way too expensive. I knew those were good arguments. We didn't like hurting animals, making noise or spending money.

So instead we used a bow and arrow. His was enormous and heavy. Mine was an exact copy, but adjusted to my size. He had made it for me in his workshop, and he showed me how to make my own arrows of pinewood and goose feathers. The wood needed to be the right thickness and flexibility to make a good arrow, he explained, and I was allowed to bend it and turn it until I started to understand what he meant. We made the arrowheads of brass from a cracked jug which I found in the pile we had named the baker's pile. 'Didn't I tell you?' he said whenever I found something in a pile. 'There's a use for everything.'

I spent weeks using tins and logs for target practice before Dad let me shoot mice in the twilight. When I finally hit one it squirmed so much that I started to cry. My arrow had gone through its bottom, right above its tail, and whenever the mouse moved the arrow and the goose feather would scrape against the ground in small jerks. Dad soon killed it completely dead with a stick. He said there was no need for me to cry, I should think instead about how pleased the fox would be to get such a meal.

We went stag hunting when the moon was out because then it was dark and light at the same time. It meant that we could see and the stag wouldn't suffer. The darkness took the pain away.

The first time I came along, the stag stood in a field right below the full moon. It had its side to us and Dad's arrow went straight into its heart. But the stag didn't fall to the ground immediately. It turned its head and looked at us and then took a few steps towards us before it knelt down in front of us. It moved slowly and it seemed quite calm. In fact, its death was one of the most peaceful things I've ever seen. I'm sure that it looked me right in the eye and that it wasn't angry.

'It was an old stag,' Dad said. 'Now there's room for one of the younger stags and we have food for several days. It's as it should be.'

'But doesn't it have children to look after?'

'They're big enough to look after themselves now.'

'When will I be big enough to look after myself?'

'Given your skill with the bow, not long.' Dad smiled, and for a moment I felt very proud and happy. But only for a moment.

'But what about you?'

'What about me?' He made a strange pause. 'I'll be with you even when you're a grown-up and can look after yourself. I'm not going to die anytime soon.'

'Not before your hair is white, right?'

'No, definitely not before my hair has gone all white.'

At that time I didn't know about Grandad and the lightning.

One of Dad's and my favourite activities was finding books for Mum because she got really happy whenever we came home with a pile of them. You wouldn't believe how many books people keep in cardboard boxes in their outhouses, and I often felt that they had never read them, or were ever going to. Eventually Mum had a mountain of books and she was definitely going to read all of them. Most were in the bedroom and in the white room, where Dad had built a big, fine bookcase for them. It's true that over time many other books and things were stacked in front of the bookcase so you couldn't see it any more – but we knew that it was there, and that was all that mattered, as we were fond of saying.

I liked books too. Mum had taught me to read and write well before my granny moved to the Head. She used to say you'd think I'd learned how before I was even born and just needed to brush up. It came easy to me, and it got even easier when I discovered how happy me reading aloud made her.

And that was why it didn't matter that my grip on the pencil was a bit odd. I held it like an arrow I was about to launch, and I simply couldn't get my head round the curved grip with my finger that Mum showed me. Finally we agreed that it was better that I held the pencil wrong and wrote right than the other way round. And if you think about it, it was lucky I didn't hold the arrow like I was meant to hold a pencil, or I wouldn't have hit my targets as often as I did.

One morning when I was practising with my bow and arrow behind the house I noticed that Mum was watching me across the laundry she was hanging up.

'I know which story we'll read next,' she said out of the blue.

Now it wasn't often that Mum said anything unless she was reading aloud from a book or trying to explain something to me. I don't think she really liked talking, but she definitely loved reading, and I loved to listen to her when we sat in her bed with a book she had chosen. In fact, I don't really know what I loved more – the stories or Mum's voice.

Sometimes I couldn't tell the difference. Sometimes I forgot the voice and disappeared into the story; other times I forgot to listen because I was lost in her voice. She didn't speak very loudly, but loud enough for a person to disappear into her voice. There was air in it. Back then.

Later, I noticed that the air disappeared. Her voice grew weaker until it was only a whisper and my name became a snatched intake of breath.

I'm glad she had time to teach me the alphabet before her voice found consonants such a problem that she could no longer use them. 'I' was the last thing she called me: 'I'. I started going to her bedroom, which she could no longer leave, and I'd read aloud to her from a book I had chosen.

One day the vowels stopped too.

I couldn't understand why she had lost her voice. She had taught me not to swallow my words when I spoke. But perhaps that was exactly what she ended up doing herself. Perhaps she ended up eating her own voice. First the air, then the sound. She ate so much.

It was *Robin Hood* she was thinking about behind the laundry.

*Dear Liv*

*I'm sure you must have wondered about my voice. I can't explain what happened to it other than the words got stuck in my throat. It felt as if they filled the space on their way up and I didn't have the strength to push them the final stretch. Finally, it was easier not to try.*

*It was like having a throat infection that you constantly try to soothe by eating hot soup and food that is easy to swallow. That was how it felt. The less I was able to say, the more I had to eat.*

*In time, a big mass of unspoken sentences was stuck in my throat. Broken words that had nothing to do with one another, interrupted beginnings, unfinished endings, lines with no air in between all piling up.*

*My grief was lodged there too. And I didn't want to pass it on to you. Or to your dad. He had his own to deal with. So I kept it inside me. It was my way of protecting you both.*

*Your dad had other ways.*

*All my love,*
*Mum*

# The Darkness and the Mess

Jens Horder took only what he needed from nature and nothing more – except when it came to resin.

It all began with his curiosity. His father had introduced him to the golden balm of the trees and told him about its properties. Shortly before his unexpected demise, Silas Horder had even demonstrated to his son how to tap the sap from a pine tree by removing a small patch of bark from the trunk. Below the patch he made a V-shaped spout which funnelled the sap into a cup which he attached below the tip of the spout.

Jens soon discovered which trees were best suited for this purpose, and in time he started tapping them regularly. He always went about it carefully because the tree should not suffer from his intrusion. It should be milked tenderly, just like a cow.

He knew that he was inflicting injury on the tree, but it felt necessary, for reasons he couldn't explain. Perhaps the resin was a kind of pine-scented high, an aromatic stimulant he couldn't do without. Or perhaps Jens genuinely believed that he would one day find a use for all the coagulated resin he kept in his workshop – a big, dark mass of irregularly shaped lumps that were reluctant to let go of one another. The sight brought back memories of a bag of stuck-together liquorice-flavoured boiled sweets that he had once shared with his father in a coffin. Nothing had ever tasted more wonderful than the sweets that night.

By experimenting, Jens had discovered a method for removing impurities from a lump of resin. He would place it on a piece of tinfoil which he stretched out over a metal tin and pierced tiny holes in. Then he melted the resin by holding it over a flame. To this end, he had made a delicate construction of iron rods and horseshoes on which the tin could stand. The impurities remained on the foil while the clean resin gathered at the bottom of the tin. Once the resin hardened, he would store it – clean resin in one barrel and discarded impurities in another. That way he could always take some and melt it again for whatever purpose he had in mind. And he had several. Resin had antibiotic properties and, with the right preparation, it could be made into soap or an excellent type of glue. It could even serve as a source of fuel. If he smeared impure resin on the top of a stick, he would have a torch that would burn reliably.

In his pocket he kept the small ant preserved in its amber universe. It looked as it had done all those years ago when Silas had first shown it to his sons on the north beach. And it looked as it had done millions of years before that. It had been that ant's task to drag tiny pieces of dried resin back to the anthill to guard it against diseases. However, it was the ant's fate to be trapped in and choked by the sticky substance and thus lose its life, if not its body.

There was something about resin which fascinated Jens

Horder. It could heal, protect and preserve. But it could also kill.

For a time, the resin barrels represented the only element of order in his workshop. The eye of the storm, you could say. They were lined up next to one another like three litter bins, yet they contained the one thing he could least do without. In the middle of this chaos of cardboard boxes, sacks, tools, engine parts, rolls of fabric, cables, food scraps, newspapers, plastic bags and items of every kind and every material, the resin barrels served as a reminder that, once, all he had cared about were the trees.

But in time even the barrels drowned under things and became impossible to spot in the workshop. Jens, however, could always find his way to them, because he navigated effortlessly through his stuff. His view of order differed from the one which might prevail among the few people who opened the door to the workshop and looked inside. Eventually no one but his wife and his daughter were allowed in. And his wife never tried.

Jens Horder's world wasn't governed by the same systems and rules that people normally subscribe to. He didn't know about dividing things up and organizing them. He knew about feelings and memories. A rasp wasn't necessarily kept beside other rasps. If the rasp was one he had dug out of a pile at the junkyard once, its natural home might end up being next to the oil lamp and a uniform jacket found in the same location. It had a logic of its own.

The scythe had its regular spot up against the big map of the island on the wall behind the lathe because its shape reminded Jens of the headland that stuck out north-east of Korsted and formed a small bay. The map was almost hidden behind some boxes now, but he knew it was there and that was all that mattered. Only the north beach could still be made out in the darkness.

Before the map became obscured, Jens had spent many hours studying it with his father. Back then the island had seemed enormous to him. Together they had concluded that it was the shape of a man's body. It had amused them to imagine Korsted as the man's heart and the junkyard as his backside and that, if they let the trees grow wild on the Head, then this man would get even wilder hair and a beard. But the man was bald on the top of his head, where the beach was. The island was a body undergoing change, and they could change it. Into a wild man.

But while the world tends to grow smaller as you yourself grow bigger, the world outside the Head only ever grew bigger for Jens. As an adult he found it increasingly overwhelming and alien as new people arrived on the main island and different types of shops, businesses and machines appeared.

Sometimes people would come to the Head and tell him that the place needed cleaning up. That the dirt was piling up. That there were too many things around him. And why didn't he start getting rid of all the rubbish?

And they would smile as they said it. That was almost the worst part.

The outside world became a threat, one which intruded on him and began to take over his life.

*

One day two women appeared in the barn and told him that he lived in an unforgivable mess, and yet there was hope because God was willing to help. God would tidy up, if Jens would love him like a father.

Jens was speechless, but he had stared hard at them and threatened them with a dung fork.

When they left, they were no longer smiling.

Jens saw something they didn't. When he studied his landscape of objects, he saw no mess or dirt. He saw an unbreakable whole. If he were to remove a single item, he would wreck the picture.

People didn't understand that everything he had accumulated had a place, a value – and a purpose. A yellowing newspaper which had served as wrapping for a clay vase could contain information which he might one day need, although he never read newspapers. An old harness reminded him of the time he had driven a horse and cart to Korsted. The torch would come in handy once he had repaired it. He had piles of batteries, and some of them must work, surely. The audio-cassette tapes definitely did. They had been taken from a pallet behind the radio shop and still lay in ruler-straight piles held together with shrink-wrapped plastic, which in turn could undoubtedly also be used for something. Tinned food was always good to have, should they ever fall on hard times, and he had never believed in 'best before' dates anyway. The smoothing plane had belonged to his father and worked impeccably. He would need the hats, should he ever wear out his grandfather's cap. The candlestick was beautiful in its symmetry; it just needed polishing. You could always use umbrellas and so never have too many of them, and he was sure that he could mend the broken ones. That someone had once thrown away a sackful of disposable cutlery seemed incomprehensible to him. Nothing was ever for single use only and one day he was going to wash it all. The sacks of salt that he had taken from a farmer's barn – the farmer tasked with gritting the roads – he would also find a use for. A better use than just chucking it on the roads.

Jens felt a deep sense of responsibility to preserve things. To keep things as they were. And he experienced joy, an emotional bond, with every single object he took into his care. This sense of connection stimulated him. And it exhausted him whenever someone tried to break it. It even frightened him.

And indeed it had gone wrong on the occasions when, for the sake of others – first his mother and later his wife – he had tried getting rid of something. He couldn't do it; it broke his heart. His mother had never understood. Nor had his beloved Maria, but she accepted him as he was and knew that it could be no other way. His father would have understood everything.

In time, a particular fear began to haunt Jens: the notion that he might inadvertently discard something irreplaceable. Something hidden among other things, underneath or inside another item. Even after everyone had stopped asking him to clear up and throw things away, this fear continued to grow. Objects and fear merged together in dreamlike scenarios and he had nightmares about overlooking a baby bird newly hatched on a piece of orange peel, a small, help-less life which would be lost were he to throw out the peel. Later, in those nightmares, the bird became a baby.

No, nothing was surplus. Despite what he taught Liv, he knew from his father, from his brother and from his son that whatever left him would never come back. And thus nothing could be allowed to leave him.

Additions, however, were frequent. For a long time they consisted of things which he himself collected; later, also things that his daughter brought home when she had been down on the main island to pick up food and other essentials. He would have preferred to go with her so that he would never have to let her out of his sight, but even-tually he was forced to trust that she would always come back.

And she did.

They had an unbreakable bond, the two of them. He knew that Liv would never leave him.

An hourglass was wedged in place horizontally in one of the carpenter's benches. Silas Horder and his younger son had found it in a barn once, brought it home to the work-shop and turned it over and over and over as they counted seconds and breaths and observed the time flow quietly but steadily through its narrow neck. For decades it had sat there in the hole, the sand evenly distributed across both sides, the dark wood and delicate glass buried under dust and memories.

Jens had watched Liv as she studied the trapped hour-glass. She knew that she wasn't allowed to touch it. Once, she had asked why they didn't use it. She so wanted to see the sand flow.

But Jens knew that time had a way of running away from you. And he couldn't bring himself to teach his daughter that lesson. Not just yet.

# December

I'm not sure how long my granny stayed with us, but I think it must have been a whole month. It was definitely in the time leading up to Christmas because she taught me to make paper hearts and to sing carols about Mary and Jesus, who I kept calling Jens. I still wasn't clear about who Jens's dad was, but I liked the idea of him being born in a stable. At night.

When I asked Mum when Carl and I were born, she replied that it must have been in the afternoon, that there had been a lady to help, and that giving birth to us had been fairly painful. I wished that she had waited until it was dark, but I was glad that at least Carl and I had been together. I'd never liked being alone.

Perhaps that explained why I liked looking at the drawings of Carl and me. They hung from a nail over the bed in the master bedroom. Dad drew them. He drew us every year when the honeysuckle blossomed, and you could tell from our faces how we had changed and yet continued to look alike. The new drawings were put on top of the old ones, so that you could flick back and forth and see how we looked as babies. I liked posing, sitting still as Dad drew me, because I could watch him and keep an eye on his hair and his beard, which was growing bigger and bigger.

Dad had also drawn Mum once. That drawing was on a wall in his workshop in a fine little clip frame. I've never seen other drawings of her. But I've also never seen a more beautiful drawing of a beautiful woman.

Although my granny had moved into the room behind the workshop, it felt as if she had taken over the main house. Carl could sense it too, but to begin with we thought it was so exciting that it never crossed our minds it might also be dangerous.

When my granny came to the bedroom and sat with me on the bed that morning, it was the first time that I spoke to an outsider, I mean properly, where it was just the two of us. For some strange reason I wasn't scared at all. Yes, to begin with, of course I was, because Mum was in the laundry room behind the barn and Dad was out by the Christmas trees, so neither of them would be able to hear me if I screamed.

But she didn't seem dangerous. The lady. She smiled and perched on the edge of the bed, and said: 'Hello, Liv, what are you doing?'

Now I thought that was a silly question; surely she could see that I was sitting in the bed, looking at the drawings.

I didn't say anything, but I pointed. Up at Carl and me.

She looked at us too. For a long time. Then she got up and walked over to us and started flicking back to when we were babies. She had her back to me.

'We look like one another,' I said.

She nodded.

'My dad did those drawings.'

She nodded again.

I stopped looking at the drawings. I started looking at the lady who I still didn't know was my granny, who was looking at Carl and me as babies. And I wondered if I should tell her about the accident.

'Something happened to my twin brother,' I said at last.

She nodded again. It really was about time she started doing something else. I wondered if perhaps she knew about Carl after all.

Finally she turned around and looked at me. She was smiling.

'Do you like pancakes?' she asked.

I had no idea what to say. I didn't know what pancakes were. And so I mimicked her.

I nodded.

I soon discovered that I liked pancakes a lot. She sprinkled sugar on the first one, then rolled it into a sausage and gave it to me while she started cooking the next. And I took a bite and I forgot to squeeze the sausage together and sugar trickled out of the end, and I could hear it sprinkling on to the floor and the lady say something. But I didn't care because it was the sweetest mouthful I had ever tasted.

She swept the floor and stroked my hair, and I got another pancake with sugar, and when I ate my fourth one I had to sit on the floor, in the middle of the sugar, and she said that it didn't matter and we started to laugh.

And then Mum came in.

The strange thing was that neither of them said anything. They just looked at one another, then Mum turned and left. She went to the barn, I think. To begin with, I didn't know whether to go with her or remain in the sugar. But then the lady started talking, and I stayed put.

'Do you have some nice friends to play with, Liv?'

I nodded. After all, I had Carl and all the animals.

She looked at me, but I didn't say anything because I had already nodded.

'I mean, do you see any other children?' she said, handing me a fresh pancake. 'Now, mind the sugar, sweetheart.'

I nodded again and reached out for the sweet roll.

'Yes, I see Carl.'

The pancake remained suspended in the air, and this time it was her fault that the sugar went everywhere. It took a moment before she gave it to me.

Carl joined us in the kitchen. He stared at the lady and I think he was a little scared of her. She looked so strange. Then again, she did have white hair. Very white.

For several days she got up and made us pancakes every morning. The first times she used ingredients from some boxes she had brought along. But when they ran out I helped by getting eggs from the chickens and milk from the cow and flour from the bags which at that point were in the hallway, I think; and those pancakes were *even* yummier because I'd helped make them.

Dad didn't eat very many and he didn't say very much. Mum ate quite a few and said nothing. I ate as many as I could.

My granny and I ended up spending a lot of time together because Mum and Dad had things to do, but I think they were really trying to avoid her. Dad was busy selling Christmas trees and driving them to the main island and running errands, and then there was the Christmas present he was making. That was why I was banned from the workshop in the last few days before Christmas. Mum was also busy doing something very secret in the bedroom.

I had no idea what they were making. The year before it was a puppet theatre and a pair of rabbit-skin gloves.

Dad had started hanging things from the living-room ceiling a long time ago so that we could move about the floor more easily. I liked sitting on the green armchair, gazing up at everything. He had made a magical cave and as the piles grew higher than the windows it got darker and darker. More and more magical.

One of my favourite things was the violin that hung from a piece of string over the wood-burning stove. When the fire was lit, the violin would twirl like a weathercock. And talking about birds, the chemist's stuffed owl would watch me from a corner. It sat on a sofa, which was on its end behind the tailor's dummy and a pile of magazines. I loved that owl. When I was out at night I practised being as quiet as it was. To be honest, it took me a while to notice that the chemist's owl was in fact a dead owl. After all, it behaved exactly like the ones I saw in the forest.

Every now and then I thought that, by now, we must surely have collected absolutely everything on the island, and yet there were always more things to bring home. For example, the day before the lady arrived Dad came back with a piano he had swapped for a Christmas tree. Some of the keys and a pedal were missing, but apart from that there was nothing wrong with it, he said. By moving some suitcases he found room for it in the living room, on the floor even. Then he placed three big radios on top of the piano – and a plaster bust of someone who was said to have played it once. This really got me thinking, because the man had no arms and no legs.

Unfortunately I got the absolutely crystal-clear impression that the lady didn't like there being so many things everywhere. She would cough – almost as loudly as she snored – when she came into the living room and she often muttered something about how what had happened in just a few years was just terrible. I had no idea what she was talking about.

She must also have been very clumsy because she kept bumping into things. One day she cried out when she bashed her big toe against the record player just inside the kitchen door. She didn't think it belonged there, even though it had been there for as long as I could remember. But that was nothing compared to the scream she let out when she bumped into the bookcase in the bathroom and a whole crate of tuna in brine came crashing down on her head. Dad came running from the workshop to see what all the fuss was about. I remember him standing in the doorway, staring at her without saying anything, and her leaning against the sink staring back at him and shaking her head. Then he left. After all, he had seen for himself that her head was still attached to her neck, it was all in working order.

After a few days she stopped looking for a cardboard

box of Christmas decorations which she felt sure had to be somewhere. Instead we made decorations from things I had found. We plaited hearts of brown paper from a roll in the scullery. They turned out amazing. I couldn't work out why she would have preferred that we made them out of differently coloured paper. What was wrong with brown? And anyway, real hearts are quite brown.

She had brought Christmas presents from the mainland, she said, and I wondered whether it might be the small radio and the board game I had found in one of her cases. The things had been carefully wrapped in very shiny paper, and after I'd examined them I wrapped them up again in the exact same way, except that I wasn't very good with the sticky tape.

When Dad brought in the tree and hoisted it up in the living room, I thought it was the finest Christmas tree I had ever seen. Carl agreed. The star that I had made from bicycle spokes glowed grey and fine right under the ceiling beam, and from the base of the trunk there was at least a metre to the floor, which left plenty of room for presents.

Christmas was a few days away, and I still didn't know that the lady was my granny. In a way, I'm a bit sad that she never got to see our go-kart. Or her own.

Sometimes I'd join her in the kitchen early in the morning, trying to find a place to sit. I wasn't scared of her, but Carl was a bit. I liked talking to her and her stroking my hair. And she smelled so nice.

She had some really exciting things in her luggage, which I spent a long time investigating when she wasn't around. Besides the presents, I found things you applied to your face, and shoes and clothes the like of which I had never seen before. Lilac nylon tights and pale brown leather shoes. I had no idea such beautiful shoes existed.

The lady was always keen to hear what I'd been up to, and so I told her what I could remember. Maybe I'd made more arrows for my bow or explored the piles of things or helped with the animals. And one morning when she asked me why I was so sleepy I mentioned that I'd been out stag hunting. I didn't mean to tell her; I'd promised Dad not to tell anyone what we did at night. We had even been extra careful with the pickup truck and left it further down the gravel road so she wouldn't hear it start.

'Do you often go out at night . . . rather than sleep?' the lady then asked me. She gave me such a strange look that Carl nudged me to make me go outside with him. But I stayed where I was.

I thought long and hard about whether now was one of those times when you had to lie.

'Carl does,' I said eventually.


I liked hearing her talk about the mainland. It sounded like the city she lived in was enormous. I imagined that there must be a huge amount of stuff in it – probably more than we could ever find room for on the Head. She also talked a lot about there being children who played together over there. And that they all went to school, where they learned to read and write and do sums.

'Tell me, Liv. Do your parents ever talk to you about you going to school? In Korsted?'

I already knew there was a school in Korsted. Sometimes

when we drove past it I saw children in the playground behind the wall. Someone was always screaming and an adult was always telling someone off. And no one carried a dagger. There was nothing in the playground except tarmac and white stripes.

Dad said that he didn't like it.

It was news to me that I was meant to go there.

'Mum has already taught me to read and write,' I said. 'And Dad is teaching me to make things from other things and turn a club on the lathe and cast sinkers and arrowheads and build a meat press and set snares and flay rabbits. And it doesn't hurt them as long as they die in the dark. And I also know the game where you go and get things without waking people up. Besides, I have a dagger, and I also play with that.'

She gave me another look and I started wondering if I had said too much. I was pretty sure I had. I wasn't used to having to watch my tongue. It was exhausting.

'I think it would be very good for you to go to school,' she said eventually. 'And leave your dagger at home.'

Now it was my turn to gawp. Carl ran to get Dad. I didn't know what to say. But she didn't seem able to stop.

'Liv, I don't think it's good for you to live here on the Head with all this rubbish and dust and dirt. You might have an accident or fall ill . . . I think it would be better for you to get away for a bit. I'll need to speak to your father about it.'

'How do you really know my dad?' I asked. I was starting to get very suspicious. Perhaps Carl had been right all along that there was something not quite right about her.

She hesitated for a second.

'Your father is my son. I'm your granny.'

That made no sense at all. And Carl wasn't there for me to check the facts with.

'It was your grandfather, my husband, Silas, who taught your father to make all those beautiful things out of wood. And the cap that your father always wears . . . it once belonged to my father.'

The pancake started to burn.

'. . . And we'll have to talk about Carl,' she went on, quickly taking the pan off the cooker.

'But he's not here,' I said, hoping that Dad and Carl would turn up soon.

'No, I know,' she said. 'But do you know where he is?'

That was the night I heard them talk in the living room while I listened behind the door. All three of them spoke, even Mum, and at some point Dad started shouting. I've never heard him shout like that before. The next morning his hair had started to turn white.

Christmas was only two days away, and very strange days they were.

No one really said anything. I think they were thinking. And so was I. About her wanting to take me with her to the mainland, about me going to school over there and meeting other children, and something about the authorities and a doctor who ought to visit and a container that she had ordered.

I clearly remember her saying that the place needed a *thorough mucking-out*. And I could understand why Dad got really upset about that, because he was always very careful to get all the muck away from the animals and out into the field where it could do some good.

Even so I found her a present. It was a small box that had a wonderful smell of tobacco. It was for keeping small things in, I thought. In the end I kept it for myself. I had found a book about butterflies for Mum, and for Dad I had collected a whole tin of resin. I also found a really beautiful red-and-yellow lump of resin, which was going to be his special present because it had a beetle inside it. If he kept it long enough, it might turn to amber, just like the lump with the ant he would usually keep in his pocket or put in a small hollow in the carpenter's bench where he kept the hourglass. I hadn't learned to count to a million years yet, but I did understand that it was a very long time.

Before my granny arrived I never wondered why we celebrated Christmas. I guess I thought we did it because it was nice. Mum and Dad never explained why, and I never asked. By talking to my granny I discovered that there was a connection between the man called Jesus and the Christmas tree and my star of bicycle spokes and our geese and the fishmonger's garden gnomes. What exactly it is, I still don't get.

Nor did I know what a container was before it arrived. This happened just after New Year. A very big lorry drove up with it on its bed. It rattled and shuddered as it came up the gravel road, and I raced round from the pump behind the barn to see what was going on. The container was set down right behind the workshop. It was a large, rectangular enclosed box of dark blue metal. Its sides came together at the top, and on one long side there were three double hatches.

'Ordered by someone called Else Horder,' I heard the man say to Dad. I don't think he realized that we had killed my granny. Then the lorry drove off without the container and the driver waved to me. It was the last time for a very long time that any outsiders saw me.

*Dear Liv*

*I don't know if it was right for us to report you dead. But we were so scared, so scared of losing you. What we did to your granny was terrible. But what she intended to do to us was even more terrible.*

*We had no choice.*

*I'm choosing to believe that we had no choice.*

*All my love,*
*Mum*

# The Killing

Deep down, Jens Horder might have known that his mother only wanted what was best for them; that her proposal was an expression of concern and love. He might even have realized that she had cause to be concerned. Nevertheless, he was incapable of interpreting Else's suggestion as anything other than a threat, a red-hot premonition of yet another unbearable catastrophe.

Maria cried when they lay together in bed that night. He hadn't seen her weep so pitifully since the accident. Since the last time his mother had been with them.

'You have to send her away,' she had sobbed. Inside her, a new life was growing. Yet another life. The other one was sleeping the sleep of the innocent in her little bedroom down the passage. With her dagger on her stomach. Alone.

It was at that moment that something snapped inside Jens: the last thread that connected him to his mother, the remains of an umbilical cord.

He clasped Maria's hand. 'Yes, I'll send her away,' he whispered as he stared up into the darkness. 'Far away. There's nothing else for it.'

She was the one person they could manage without.

'I'll do it before Christmas.'

*

His wife heard the words he whispered. She understood exactly what he meant. And she knew that she should protest. But she couldn't.

Jens got up from the bed, leaned over Maria and kissed her forehead before he got up and got dressed. Then he disappeared.

Soon afterwards, she could hear him working in his workshop.

★

Else Horder also heard him from the white room where she, contrary to her usual habit, had yet to fall asleep.

She concluded that Jens must be finishing some last-minute Christmas presents, but even so it was odd for him to be working in the middle of the night. Then again, there was very little her younger son could do these days that would shock her. He and his little family seemed to live in a world of their own, where everything was chaos. Else knew about isolation better than anyone, including how it could mess with your head, but this . . . this was serious.

She couldn't help but feel a little guilty. Not for all of it, of course, but still. And though it broke her heart, she no longer had any doubts that she had to save Liv from the fate she was being dragged into. The girl didn't appear to have been seen by a doctor for years, because her parents 'didn't like doctors and that kind of thing', and Else suspected that the girl had never played with, or possibly even spoken to, another child. It was true that Maria was academically inclined, but she was unlikely to be able to home-school a child, as she claimed she wanted to. Liv had to be desperate to get out and meet other people – people who weren't busy eating themselves to death or turning their home into a junkyard. There was nothing normal in the poor girl's life.

And then there were the night-time excursions, which worried Else, not to mention the business with Carl. Truth be told, the whole thing might end up a matter for the police, a tragic case. If that happened, she could only hope that they didn't start asking questions about the accident and reopen old wounds. That was the last thing anyone needed.

Something had to give, and Else had set the process in motion by ordering and paying for a skip, which would arrive just after New Year. Jens hadn't suspected that anything was amiss. He had just dropped her off at the post office one day and picked her up a little later, as they had arranged. With some help from the post-office lady, Else had found a skip company, called it from the post-office telephone and sent them a cheque immediately. It was pricey, but necessary, Else thought. She knew that the cheque wouldn't bounce because her ever-helpful cousin had insisted on making a contribution towards unforeseen expenses. Else was sure that Karen would understand about the skip, if only she could get in touch with her. Else was starting to worry. Karen wasn't answering her phone. She hoped nothing bad had happened to her.

As for ordering the skip behind Jens's back, Else didn't feel entirely comfortable about that; she was aware this would be seen as serious meddling. But once the skip arrived surely it would represent an opportunity, she thought, to start clearing up and to bring a breath of fresh air into the house. Perhaps it was the only way she could help her son out of his chaos.

Else would have loved nothing more than to stay on and help out for as long as it took, but she didn't have much faith that she would be allowed to. She had resigned herself to thinking that perhaps it would be better if she wasn't there to interfere.

But she couldn't be so passive when it came to Liv. Else had decided to contact the authorities, but not until the New Year. For now, they would just have to try to make the most of Christmas.

When she finally managed to rid herself of her troubling thoughts and fall asleep, she did so to the sounds of constant sawing and hammering in the workshop next door.

The night before Christmas Eve they ate in silence. Else had insisted on shopping and cooking, and she had an inkling that she had only been permitted to do so because Jens's jaw was so clenched that he was incapable of replying with anything other than a nod.

She had tried and failed to catch her son's eye all day. Once he had helped himself to a cup of coffee that morning, he kept well out of her way. As had Maria. She had clammed up like an oyster and didn't say even good morning when she came downstairs, but her red and swollen eyes were evidence that she had had a troubled night. During the day Else could hear her potter about the house, and she saw her move laboriously around the barn, but she never showed herself in the kitchen. That was probably just as well; given how little space there was, the two of them were unlikely to fit in at the same time. Liv came and went, but even she seemed as if she didn't know what to do with herself. At one point, Else watched her disappear into the forest with her bow across her back. She didn't come back for several hours.

This reminded Else of a time when she had stood in the same kitchen, watching her sons disappear in between the same trees. In those days Mogens was always the one who returned first, and he would usually be heading purposefully towards the workshop with some new idea in his head. Jens would stay away for so long that she would get worried. When he finally came back and she asked him what he had been doing, all he would say was that he had been with the trees. Silas had never worried about him.

They were having meatloaf for dinner. Jens had loved his mother's meatloaf ever since he was a boy, and Else harboured a slender hope that he might sense her goodwill through the food.

If he did, he hid it well. He ate, but apparently more out of hunger or habit than pleasure. Else wasn't even sure that he noticed what he was eating because he stared at the table most of the time and moved his fork without looking at it. He seemed to have aged greatly overnight.

No one was interested in the bottle of wine on the table.

Maria also ate her dinner, but as usual without saying a

word, and she completely ignored the fact that Liv was poking at the meatloaf suspiciously and sorting pieces of carrot, leek and onion into small piles on her plate so that quite a lot of the meatloaf dropped on to the tablecloth.

Else was about to rebuke the girl when she realized that, if she did, those might be the only words spoken at dinner and so she changed tack. 'Are you looking forward to Christmas, Liv?' she asked her granddaughter instead.

Liv looked up from the chaos that was unfurling on her plate. She nodded and smiled for a moment like a child who looks forward to Christmas. Oh, thank God, a glimpse of normality, Else thought, and returned her smile.

There were no protests when Else volunteered to clear the table and wash up. It seemed everyone had expected her to. In a matter of seconds Jens and Maria had retired to the workshop and bedroom respectively, and Liv was playing in the living room. Else could hear the child chattering to herself.

Before she retired to her own room, she drank a glass of wine at the kitchen table. She had done the dishes, but it was a kitchen which was impossible to clean. The darkness penetrated everywhere.

She started to cry.

Outside, an owl hooted.

★

When Jens told his daughter that darkness swallowed up all pain, he hadn't been completely untruthful. He felt more comfortable in the darkness, when it enveloped him in its warm embrace. Somewhere in his memories he felt his father's arms in the coffin, his warm breath against his neck, the scent of freshly planed wood. Understanding, trust, safety.

Jens knew exactly where everything was in their bedroom when it was dark. He didn't want to wake Maria, so he slipped carefully out of bed without turning on the light or stepping on the books or bumping into the sewing machine or the empty aquarium or a single one of the boxes which pretty much blocked the path from the bed to the door. And he moved quietly along the passage, down the stairs, through the hallway, and out through the front door.

The workshop lay diagonally in front of him like a rectangular shadow in the early dawn. The white room, where his mother was asleep, was at the far end. He had never thought how misleading the name 'white room' had grown over time. Of all the things to come into his mind at this moment.

A cold wind blew from the forest, carrying with it a few snowflakes, like a fleeting premonition of a white Christmas. He gasped, a little startled, when he stepped on a small spruce decoration which had blown from the nail on the door to the white room. He wasn't used to there being anything on the ground in that spot. The pillow with which he intended to suffocate his mother was tucked under his arm.

The door wasn't locked. Else and Silas had never bothered locking the doors on the Head, and Jens wondered whether she ever locked her door in town. All those people. Someone might turn up and do something, take something.

He always locked the door.

He could hear loud snoring from the bed. It was a familiar sound to Jens, and he found it both comforting and repellent. Right now, it was helping him by acting as a sort of beacon and an assurance that his mother was fast sleep. He stepped cautiously inside and closed the door behind him with a faint click. He stood very still for several minutes, listening to her snoring while his eyes adjusted to the darkness inside. Contours slowly started to emerge, including the outline of his daughter getting up noiselessly from the other side of the bed.

'Liv?' he whispered. 'What are you doing here?'

Liv walked across to her father with silent footsteps, and he knelt down in front of her so they were at eye level.

'I'm practising for when I next go out at night,' she whispered enthusiastically. 'I'm getting really good, Dad. Look at all the stuff in her bags. There's so much.'

Then she put her hand on his knee. 'But what are you doing in here?' she asked, with a puzzled look at the pillow. 'Are you going to sleep here?'

'No, but I . . .' Jens hesitated. Sending her away felt wrong. In some inexplicable sense it even seemed right that she was there. She was used to being involved in everything.

'Liv, do you remember how killing the old stag was the right thing to do?'

She nodded eagerly.

'At this moment in time, killing your granny is the right thing to do.'

Jens studied his daughter's face. Her eager nodding was instantly replaced by complete immobility. He could see her shining eyes.

'OK,' she said at last. Her whisper had taken on a pensive quality it hadn't had before. Something not entirely childlike, something approaching an adult understanding. 'But why?'

'She has lived a long and good life, and she's ready to move on.'

'Yes, but . . . I mean, she's your *mum*? She told me so the other day, and you said that it was true.'

'Yes.'

'Is it all right to kill your mum?'

'Liv, if I don't do it, she'll take you away from us. Then you wouldn't live here any more. Your mum and I wouldn't be able to cope with that . . . Would you?'

Liv shook her head firmly. Over in the bed the deep snoring continued with soothing regularity.

Then Liv placed her hands on her father's shoulders, leaned towards him and whispered into his ear.

'Then I guess you'd better do it.'

Jens put his arm around his daughter and planted a soft kiss on her cheek. 'Right, darling,' he whispered. 'I'll do it so quickly that she won't feel a thing.'

'And besides, it's dark.'

Jens nodded, released his hold of her and slowly got up.

'But, Dad,' Liv whispered, grabbing his arm, 'how are you going to do it?'

There was silence for a moment. Total silence, because Else Horder's snoring had suddenly stopped. Now they could hear the faint sound of snowflakes striking the wall like soft crystals.

They heard her stir, pull the duvet over her and exhale a sigh, which could be anything between sleeping and being awake.

They waited.

Finally her breathing grew heavier, until it culminated in the usual deep inhale.

And Jens finally answered his daughter.

'I'll do it with this.' He grabbed the pillow firmly. Then he looked at Liv again. He could see her clearly in the darkness now, but he was aware that she could see him even more clearly. Her night vision was impressive. 'Perhaps you had better leave?'

'No, I want to be here.' she replied without hesitation. Liv could be very strong-minded.

Jens felt a strange joy in his stomach. He wanted her to be there, this little spirit who always made him feel less alone in the world. He was glad that they would have this together, just like all the other things they shared.

'Then go and stand over there,' he whispered, and nodded towards the far end of the bed. 'Don't get too close. She'll probably flop about a bit.'

'Like the flounders?'

'Yes, just like the flounders.'

Else Horder lay on her back with her hands folded on

top of her duvet as if in prayer. It was almost as if she had heard their conversation and wanted to make the job easier for her son.

It took only a moment.

Meanwhile, her granddaughter clutched an invisible hand in the darkness.

*I didn't know you were there until you told me so afterwards. You were never meant to be. I think I would have stopped him, had I known that you would be there.*

*But then, it had to be done. It was our only way out.*

*I want you to know, Liv. You are not an accomplice in this, even though you witnessed it. But I am. My only wish was to be left in peace. I knew what he had planned and I did nothing to stop him. More than anything it was my wishing which drove him to do it. He's not a killer, Liv.*

# The Newcomer

The pub in Korsted was situated in the bend of the road right after the butcher's and the undertaker's when leaving the town heading north. It wasn't a big pub, but it had been the only one on the island since the pub in the south was turned into a village store. During the winter months most of the rooms were empty, but loyal regulars made sure to keep the business alive. The islanders didn't want to lose their local. Not only was the food in a class of its own, the pub also served a variety of other purposes: it was the social hub for this part of the island. It was where you would cycle to use the telephone, if you were one of those people who had yet to have one of their own installed, but more importantly people would stop by to catch up on the latest discreetly uttered gossip or to watch the colour television in the back room. Especially on Saturdays, when the pools football matches were on. Whenever the landlord rang the bell to signal that a goal had been scored in an English League game, it was time for another round in the public bar.

The pub held the locals together and the half-timber held the red bricks together, even those that were starting to crumble. The thatched roof was surely good for another twenty years or so, people thought. It was good straw. But the landlord really ought to clear the moss on the north side before the moisture got through.

Roald had taken over the pub when his uncle died suddenly of a heart attack. The opportunity had come as a godsend. When his aunt's letter lay open on the kitchen table in his flat on the mainland, he realized that the feeling that had been nagging him these last few years could now be addressed. She was pleading with him, but without expecting a yes. *I don't want to sell the pub before I've asked you, Roald.*

It was purely a question of daring: take the leap, man up, quit his job, pack his stuff, drive the car to the port and take the small ferry to a new life. He was divorced; they had no children and so there was no issue of custody. Sadly. If only his sperm had been more cooperative, he might have had both children and his wife today.

Now she was the mother of two small cherubs and irritatingly happy with a long-haired national treasure who sang sentimental songs about love and world peace. Roald hated himself for hating him.

As a desperate countermove Roald had decided to marry his job. He taught at a sixth-form college. It wasn't a terribly happy arrangement, but it had the obvious advantage that it helped pass the time. In truth, his time was swallowed up by lesson planning, homework marking, staff meetings and inane gossip about the head teacher's new house and his colleagues' affairs with one another.

In time a small scab began to form on his wound.

If only it could get a little more air, this scab would

harden and fall off. He was sure of it. And that was the thought which had been nagging him. He needed air. Any kind of air except the one inside the staff room or indeed anywhere in the whole town. That air was filled with smoke, and school routines ground him into the tarmac so that he had to drag himself, wheezing, up to his third-floor flat with his shopping bags and guilty conscience about the cigarettes and the whisky and all the lovely girls he didn't have the energy to invite home and undress. He was starting to regret the time he never took, the delicious food he never cooked, the good books he never read, the dreams he could no longer remember. It was as if it had all come to nothing.

There was only one answer.

★

The ferry man with the grey beard scrutinized Roald discreetly when he declined the offer of a return ticket. His gaze also took in the car which was packed to the rafters with bags, a house plant, books, a ladder bookcase that had split and yellowed in the places where the books hadn't kept the wood virgin pale. On the passenger seat was a box with a radio and a stack of cassette tapes. Was the driver of this car being categorized as the lost townie he was or deemed a potential asset for the island?

The ferry man gave nothing away. He merely took the money Roald passed through the car window and stuffed it into the black money belt he wore around his waist, then pointed backwards to the open deck with one hand and waved the next car forward with the other. The rust-red metal ramp rattled under the Simca when the new publican drove on board.

On a lonely road with crops as far as the eye could see, Roald stopped the car and got out. The warm island air hit him as if the sky had slipped into his lungs in that moment and inflated them. Soon the scent found its way to that place in his nose which harbours the strongest memories and tickled him with feather-light reminiscences of bicycle rides and cows and grown-ups skimming stones along the water's edge and eating freshly caught fish as the sun went down.

He lay down on his back in a sea of barley and glowing poppies and took everything in. A lark singing energetically suddenly filled the world. He spotted it eventually, a tiny flickering dot suspended high up in the blue, carrying the whole sky.

They got used to him after a few years. The regulars.

They had turned up at the reopening, and his aunt's heartfelt introduction of her nephew had evidently worked wonders. It was clear that she was well liked. And it was just as clear that the locals were sad that she was moving to the mainland to be near her family. But all those grandchildren exerted a strong pull, and her rheumatism was wearing her down. And she missed Oluf. People understood.

However, they didn't understand why Roald arrived on his own. Divorce wasn't done on the island. You stuck it out and slept in separate bedrooms if it made things easier and the house was big enough. You would never discuss personal problems openly, and certainly not with people you didn't know well. Any talk of private matters would happen only between trusted friends, and confessions would limit themselves to a few muffled words that didn't reveal too much.

For that same reason, it might not have been Roald's smartest move to introduce himself as a divorced sixth-form teacher and talk frankly about how his open marriage hadn't worked out. Perhaps he shouldn't have revealed that he was thinking of writing a novel one day either, or that he was partial to skinny-dipping. But at the time he had thought it wise to lay his cards on the table from day one so that they knew what they were dealing with. Today he would have left most of it out.

Even so, the locals had given him a chance – mainly because they had nowhere else to meet. And in time they began to accept him. He even suspected a couple of them harboured considerable sympathy for him. It was mutual.

His undeniably best move on that first evening had been to assure them that everything would carry on as before, that the chef would be staying and that not as much as a comma would be changed on the menu, though the menu would, frankly, have benefited from having its punctuation revised and the 'G' replaced with a 'C' in 'Gordon Bleu'. But irrespective of the spelling, the food was truly excellent, and the chef was a nice guy who didn't say very much but one to whom laughter came easily. He turned out to be a distant cousin of Roald's, but Roald didn't realize it until the chef mentioned it the following year.

*

Roald could never prove if the break-ins started when he moved in or if they were a continuation of thefts which had occurred in Oluf's time.

When he questioned his aunt delicately on the telephone she replied that Oluf had never mentioned anything about break-ins, but he had wondered at the rapid depletion of the stock room at times. She sounded somewhat anxious at the question, and Roald quickly dismissed it as insignificant and distracted her with an update about the undertaker's gout.

Roald, however, continued to ponder it. And one day he discovered how the thief had got in. Only it didn't make things any less bizarre.

*Dear Liv*

*When I was a child in the bookshop I had an invisible friend called John Steinbeck. When my parents were too busy to take care of me or I felt sad at school, he would keep me company.*

*All the time I was at school I was only sent outside the classroom once, and that was because John Steinbeck suddenly poked out his head between my English teacher's legs, while she was asking me questions about* Of Mice and Men, *which you must read. I couldn't help laughing and, once I had started, I couldn't stop. My English teacher got hysterical because I kept staring at her legs. As I lie here, the memory can still make me laugh.*

*From that day onwards my classmates made even more fun of me, but I think it frustrated them that they never discovered my secret.*

*I've never told a soul about my invisible friend, but I have a hunch that I can tell you.*

*All my love,*
*Mum*

# Carl and the Game

Carl was always with me when I went out at night. It was good to have someone to talk to once Dad could no longer come with me. He had to stay at home and look after the house and the things and Mum, he said, so now it was my turn to take care of the other business. I didn't tell him that I brought Carl along. After all, I was supposed to be doing it on my own.

Carl was everything I wasn't. Or didn't want to be. Like scared. Scared of people who didn't live on the Head, scared of not being able to find enough things for Dad and not enough food for Mum, scared of making a noise, scared of being caught, scared of going out when it was daylight, and scared of everything that was hiding in the dark. And scared to admit that he was scared. He would only ever tell me.

But he could also get sad.

And angry.

He could get really cross with Mum, say, because she ate so much and moved so little and grew so big that we wondered whether the floor was strong enough to hold her. After all, there was so much stuff upstairs in the bedroom – and Mum in addition to it all. Sometime after my granny's death, Dad started sleeping in the white room to give Mum more space in the double bed, seeing as she spent all her time there.

I don't really understand how she grew so fat. Yes, she

ate a lot, but not that much, and it wasn't cakes and things like that all the time. Sometimes it could just be a loaf of white bread that I'd brought back. And veal chops from the pub. And cheese and ham and potatoes and carrots and frozen peas that melted on the way home.

No, it was as if the food grew once it was inside her. And yet she asked for more. That, in particular, drove Carl crazy. But he would also get sad because our mum really was the sweetest mum we could imagine, and once she had been the most beautiful woman in the whole world, or at least on the island. Now all that was about to disappear inside her behind pillows of fat, and her eyes no longer shone like they did in Dad's drawing. I think that her beauty and her glow were trapped along with all the words somewhere in her stomach where they were waiting to be set free. But you can't cut open your own mum's stomach, can you?

Carl and I would talk about it. Why you couldn't just make a hole and cut away everything that wasn't necessary, so that she would be freed of everything that weighed her down and become her old self again. But we weren't sure that you could cut into someone who was alive without her being no longer alive afterwards. The very last thing we wanted was that she would stop being alive. And we didn't want to hurt her either.

I very nearly persuaded Carl to ask Dad about it one day, but he didn't dare. And I don't think Dad would have listened anyway; he never listened to Carl.

And if I'm being totally honest, I knew that Dad couldn't see him. Only I could.

*

Carl was, I could feel, a bit annoyed that they hadn't taken better care of him when he was little. And though I could see him and hear him and play with him most of the time, it was a bit like he was missing. If nothing else, it would have been nice if he could have helped me carry things, because my bag could be very heavy when we walked back home at night.

The pub was our favourite place. Carl and I often didn't get any further than the pub because it pretty much had everything we needed. Dad did warn me not to go there too often. I wouldn't want to get caught, would I?

He used to go there lots in the past, but it got too difficult for him when they began locking the back door. But there was always a basement window left a little bit open at night, and it overlooked the back. It was too small for Dad, but I could just about squeeze through it. In time I got very good at easing the hook off the hasp and opening the window enough to wiggle through, feet first, getting a foothold on the radiator and jumping from there on to the floor without making a sound. The window led to a small corridor and from that you could get into the stock room or go up some steps to the kitchen.

I always brought my smallest torch, but I was very careful about using it, especially in the kitchen, where one of the windows could be seen from the road. It was better to wait for my eyes to get used to the darkness, to try to be like the owl. My eyes had grown so used to darkness that in time I saw best at night.

I would take all sorts of things from the stock room.

Mainly tins and toilet paper, but sometimes also food from the big freezer. If there were any sweets, I'd always take some because Mum loved sweets. As I mostly picked bags with small pieces, liquorice pastels and gummy bears, say, I didn't think that they could be making her fat. I also tried very hard to bring back biscuits because there was something very special about eating biscuits in bed with Mum. We would always break and shake them before we ate them. 'So the calories can fall out,' she would say. That made us laugh.

But, to be honest, I never really understood what she meant. I never saw any calories fall on to the duvet, the books or the other things. Nevertheless, I would always snap and shake my biscuits. I still do. They taste much better that way.

Every time I would remember to peek inside the fridge in the pub kitchen and I'd often find foil trays with food that was already cooked. Sometimes I'd take them out and hold them for a long time, breathing in the smell of the food. At times I might taste a bit as I stood there, even put a few trays in my bag. But I had to be very careful and never leave the fridge door open for a long time, Dad said. There was a light inside it, and someone might see it through the window. There were no curtains.

The thought of light and noises that might give me away terrified me. Darkness and silence were my friends.

I never took too much at any one time. That was the whole point of the game. Otherwise I might get caught, and that was the worst outcome imaginable. Not only because it would put an end to the game, but also because I didn't know what they might do if they caught me. The strangers.

To begin with, I thought the game was just for fun, but in time I realized that we played it in order to survive. And that the consequences of being caught were unbearable. In time I realized that this game was deadly serious.

Dad spoke about them, the others. That, yes, they took part in the game, but not in a nice way. The strangers hoped to spot us so that they could do nasty things to us. Carl and I wished that he had never told us because it was hard not to think about it when we were off on our own. The thought would make Carl's heart beat so hard that I could hear it.

One day when I asked Dad if we couldn't just stop the game, he said something I'll never forget: 'But then your mum would starve to death, and I would be sad.'

He gave me such a strange look as he said it.

It was at that moment that I finally noticed what was happening to his face. His beard had grown enormous. Before, I thought that it looked like the undertaker's larch hedge just after he trimmed it. And that it was lovely and soft to touch. Now Dad's beard looked more like a pile of twigs. It was dry and black and white at the same time, and a few wood shavings and bits of cobwebs were trapped in it. I even spotted something stirring inside the beard – possibly an animal trapped in the cobweb, or maybe it was just his mouth moving. His hair had also grown long and strange, and his eyebrows were so bushy they looked a bit scary.

But the weirdest and the worst were the eyes staring at me from under the bushy brows. They were staring without seeing, like a milky layer was covering the kindest eyes I knew. It was as if I couldn't see Dad any more.

That day the responsibility on my shoulders truly dawned on me. How much depended on what I dragged home in my bag. That day I became big in a very small way because I still had to fit through the basement window in the pub.

Whenever I was in the pub kitchen I always looked around for things that Dad might like. There were all sorts of things in the drawers, and I usually found something for him. It might be a tea towel. Or a soup ladle. Or a roll of cling film or possibly an egg slicer. I didn't always know what something was, but if I liked the look and the feel of it I was sure Dad would too.

The strangest thing I ever found on my trips was a long thingy under a bed in a holiday cottage. There were batteries inside it, but you didn't have to take them out and press them against your tongue to make it buzz. You could just press your tongue against the thingy itself, push the button and the whole thing would vibrate! Dad told me it was a kitchen utensil, for making eggnog. But when I tried it out I was very disappointed with the result.

Every now and then I managed to sneak one of the pub's pots or pans into my bag. I had to be especially careful with them, Dad said. It was best only to take things people wouldn't notice were missing, at least not immediately. But when I dragged home one half of the kind of bicycle which comes apart in the middle he couldn't hide his excitement, and he begged me to fetch the other half as soon as I could.

And so I did. And when I realized how happy bicycles made him, I started finding even more. All kinds. It was easy, because I didn't have to climb inside people's houses to get them. Bicycles were usually left in places where they were easy to take and, if they were unlocked, it was easy peasy. Carl didn't really like cycling, so I pushed them home across the Neck. For his sake.

But I've got ahead of myself. Before all of that, before Mum got so fat that she could no longer leave the bedroom, and before Dad stayed at home on the Head at night to look after the things, and before I noticed the cobweb in his beard. *Before* all of that, other things happened.

Such as me getting a baby sister.

# The Dead and the Newborn

Maria and Jens Horder reported their daughter missing shortly after the New Year. Sadly, there was every reason to fear that she had drowned in an accident. Jens Horder himself went to the police officer in Korsted to tell him what had happened. Or rather what he assumed had happened:

Liv had been out playing on her own the day before. There was nothing unusual about that. She was used to being out in the fields and the surrounding forest, and she had never given them any cause to worry. However, yesterday she hadn't come home in the afternoon, as she usually did. When it started getting dark Jens had searched all over the Head for her. Liv would never leave the Head on her own, he assured the police officer. He was afraid that Liv might have fallen and hurt herself in the forest, and he didn't want to abandon his search and drive to the main island until he was absolutely sure that he had looked everywhere she might possibly be. His wife, Maria, had also searched. Though mostly in and immediately around the house.

Jens Horder had gradually extended his search, he said, and eventually got as far as the north beach, though he didn't think that Liv would have gone there on her own, as she knew perfectly well that she was not allowed.

143

Nevertheless, there were signs to indicate that she had been there: when Jens Horder had examined the shore in the darkness, Liv's beloved leather wristband had appeared in the beam of his torch. It had been lying, half buried, in the sand in front of the small wooden jetty where their dinghy was moored; or rather, should have been moored. Jens Horder had not in his wildest imagination thought that Liv might walk as far as the deserted beach and then dare venture out in the dinghy on her own. But she was, he had to admit, a stubborn little soul, and once she set her heart on something, it took almost supernatural powers to change it. Earlier that day she had pestered him to go sailing, but he had said no. It was far too cold for a little girl like her to go sailing in January.

Now, however, it looked like she had taken matters into her own hands. And, tragically, she had chosen to do so on a day when a strong wind had started blowing from the west.

As Jens Horder explained how he had searched the shore the officer felt the father's terror and envisioned the foaming waves crashing on to the beach like grey-white explosions in the dark. He had a daughter the same age as Liv. He, too, had been out last night and heard how the wind tore through the high street and seen how every now and then the fast-moving clouds would reveal an icy moon. To imagine a child alone at sea underneath that moon – your own child . . .

He studied Jens Horder, who he hadn't seen much of in the last few years. Once, way back when, they had sat in the same little schoolroom, but after his father's sudden death it hadn't proved possible to make Jens attend regularly, and one day he simply stopped turning up. Since then the school had moved to new and better premises and the teaching staff had expanded. The officer's own daughter would be starting school soon.

He had caught only the odd glimpse of Jens Horder's young daughter, whom he kept mistaking for a boy, in the pickup truck with her father. It had caused him to reflect on how isolated a life she must live on the Head. For that same reason he had toyed with the idea of driving up there with his own daughter to say hello. Just to see how they were. People on the island valued their privacy, and it was well known that the Horder family especially didn't welcome visitors – but even so, seeing as they had a child? Judging by the size of the girl in the pickup truck, he had surmised that the children would start school together.

But it was not to be.

Jens Horder told the police officer that he had eventually found the dinghy further up the coast, where the island meets the sea with big boulders and a steep slope up to the forest. His heart broke when he spotted the empty boat wedged in between two big boulders, having apparently drifted eastwards with the current. The stern was under water. Not far from there he had seen one oar in the waves, which had sucked it out into the darkness, only to hurl it back to the shore like a lost lance. At least that was how the officer imagined the scene. The current in that location was known to be dangerous.

Horder had managed to free the dinghy from the stones

but lost it again when the current pulled it back out. He had called out for his daughter over and over, he said, and he had shone his strong torch at every inch of coastline. But there were no footprints anywhere to give him even the slightest hope that a child had crawled ashore.

He had searched the whole night until the sun had finally risen but had found nothing but a painfully familiar rabbit-skin glove which had been washed ashore. Again, the police officer could imagine the scene: how the glove had looked at the water's edge, dark and glossy, like a drowned animal. The black despair that must have consumed Jens Horder when he realized its significance.

At last the desperate father had given up his search and returned to his wife with the devastating news. And now he was standing in front of the officer in his old coat, wrapped in woollen scarves and a shabby cap which looked like something from another age. His face was sunken and pale, and the beard he had grown in recent years made him look considerably older than he was. Not least because both his beard and hair had become remarkably grey this winter. The police officer had noticed it when he had bumped into Horder just after Christmas. People were even talking about it in the village store. How Jens Horder had suddenly gone grey.

And now this.

His prematurely aged hand clutched a small leather wristband.

'We need to send a team out to look for her,' the police officer said in a voice alien even to him. 'I'll contact the mainland right away. Perhaps they can dispatch a helicopter.'

He could see from the anguished face in front of him that his words did not rouse any hope at all.

'I know my daughter,' Jens Horder said. 'If she was alive, I would know.'

He was a man who knew with absolute certainty that he had lost his only child. He hadn't come to report her missing; he had come to report her dead.

When the police officer realized this he experienced a moment of all-consuming despair, as if he were the grieving father. He tried to pull himself together and play his role with the calm that it demanded. But everything he did or said felt wrong. In an attempt to show his sincere sympathy, he accidentally smiled. It was totally misplaced. It was a smile that had gone astray, and it was doomed because it didn't belong in this moment. It had no place faced with this man and his tragedy.

But Jens Horder saw it.

'Is your mother still visiting you, Jens? I saw her in town just before Christmas,' the officer said, while the smile was dragged into a muddy darkness like a fawn in quicksand. His usually steady hand shook as he scribbled down a few lines on a notepad. *Presumed drowned. North beach.* With his other hand he tried to hide his trembling chin.

'No, she went back. Before New Year.'

They dispatched a helicopter. People searched everywhere along the coast and in the forest, down along the Neck and the northern part of the main island.

Meanwhile, Liv Horder sat as quiet as a mouse in a locked skip behind her father's workshop. Hidden behind cardboard boxes and tyres and newspapers and magazines and toys and sand bags and sacks of salt and sinks and blank cassette tapes and broken tools and gas flasks and crispbread and paint and bags of sweets and second-hand clothing and stacks of books and piles of blankets and things, all of which someone had lost and briefly wondered where it might have gone before soon forgetting all about it.

★

The parents didn't want a memorial service. Nor did they want to be contacted by compassionate, nosy people from the main island, or a visiting psychologist who wanted to help them process their grief.

The parents wanted to be left in total peace.

And when the authorities' envoy finally left, with a certain degree of horror at the messy conditions under which the poor girl must have lived, calm descended on the Head once more. Jens Horder put up a barrier where the gravel road took a sharp bend to the left before it continued a fair stretch up towards the house. And next to the barrier he put up a post box and a slightly bigger wooden box.

*No entry* read a new sign.

Not: *No trespassing.* Just *No entry.* That meant absolutely no one.

Should someone decide to defy the sign and follow the path around the barrier, they would soon encounter a tripwire, just one of many traps which from now on would safeguard the Horder family against unwanted intrusion.

*

These were bright months, despite the winter being as black as night. No one sent official letters about Liv having to start school. No one asked questions about the envelope from M which hit the bottom of their post box at the end of each month, regular as clockwork.

Jens Horder continued to pay any bills which, if left unpaid, would attract unwanted visitors. People noticed him when he turned up at the post office. Not because he drew attention to himself, he pretty much didn't open his mouth, but because an unpleasant smell lingered about him, and his clothes bore evidence of not having been washed recently.

In the past people had admired his beautiful if rather odd shirts, which his wife made for him. And when the chemist's mother, right up until her death, insisted that the back of Jens Horder's shirt matched that of her missing slip, it was attributed to the old lady's increasing dementia. After the tragic drowning accident, however, people only ever saw Jens Horder wear the same faded, grey sweater which was badly in need of washing and defluffing from pilling and wood shavings, just as his corduroy trousers were in desperate need of patching. He no longer changed his shoes but seemed comfortable in a pair of old rubber wellingtons whose shafts, for reasons unknown, he had rolled down, but he never bothered kicking the mud off before stepping inside. The cap was the same as always, even though a compassionate farmer had given him a new one.

Only the smell changed. And every time for the worse.

The two women who took turns being behind the till started arguing over who would serve him when they saw the pickup truck pull up outside. And customers in the queue started letting him walk straight to the front so that he would leave as quickly as possible. Anyone who didn't know him would scrunch up their nose and wonder who this oddball was. And those who did know Jens Horder would exchange sad, knowing looks. Some tried to greet him amicably as he walked past, but they never got more than a fleeting smile in return, and in time the silent smile was reduced to a stare at the post-office floor.

The postman who served the Head also noticed the change. He had been used to delivering the sparse post to the house and would occasionally depart with a few letters from Jens or Maria to post, but now he had to settle for the impersonal post box down where the road bent. If there were parcels, a rare occurrence, he was to put them in the wooden box next to it. And if he had any messages for the couple, they should also be left in the box. A pen and paper had been left there for that very purpose.

The postman was especially intrigued by the barrier that had been put up, but as he himself was from a rather eccentric family on the main island, he didn't regard the device as wholly out of the ordinary. He was convinced that he was the illegitimate son of the renowned and very handsome postmaster Nielsen from Korsted and not the ugly cross-eyed farmer who had raised him. That is to say, the postman had a certain appreciation for rumours as well as for family secrets.

He hoped that one day he would deliver a parcel that needed a signature to the Head so that he would have a reason to cross the barrier. As a postman, he was not only dutiful by nature – come rain, come shine, and so on – but also incurably nosy. Besides, he was desperate to bring news of the Horders to his friends at the pub. Not that he was a gossip, heaven forbid, but being able to imply that he knew something the others didn't would make him very happy. It was a source of great anguish that he had not yet succeeded in convincing his friends, discreetly of course, of his real ancestry. He couldn't say anything outright; it wasn't the done thing. But he could hint, and he kept dropping hints, as if his life depended on it, without anyone so much as raising an eyebrow.

Liv knew that not being seen was a matter of life and death, so whenever she had the slightest suspicion that someone was coming, she would disappear, quick as lightning and without a sound, into the furthest corner of the container. Here, with her father's help, she had made a wonderful little den for herself behind tyres and cardboard boxes. Two big duvets and a whole pile of blankets kept her warm, but should she get cold in spite of that, there was a sack of extra-warm clothing which she could help herself to. She also had books and torches and plenty of batteries and sweets, crackers and bread and bottles of water, so she wanted for nothing.

To begin with, while everyone was searching for her, she hadn't dared to switch on the torches. Instead she had lain quietly under her duvet in pitch darkness, listening out for the faintest sound. In the constant darkness she had lost track of time, and it wasn't long before she couldn't tell whether it was day or night. Soon the darkness also started to feel heavy in her eyes and lungs.

She was missing Carl, who wouldn't join her.

Finally, after far too much time, he came. She didn't see him, but she knew that he was there with her in the silence. She didn't dare talk to him, due to the risk of being overheard, but he whispered to her that he was there – and that he was scared of the strangers, of the darkness, of time, of uncertainty, of the air. And the smell, which enveloped them like a thick blanket of old rubber and dust and mould and dried-out paint and turpentine rags.

His fears made her calm down. She comforted Carl without a word, and felt stronger than she was. As long as she focused her attention on reassuring her twin brother, fear would not take hold of her.

They lay like this for a long time, she and Carl, surrounded by the darkness, which was surrounded by things, which were surrounded by a sealed metal container. They thought about the air outside, the scent of the forest, and tried to pull it deep into their den, through the thick blanket and right into their lungs.

Eventually they heard sounds, they heard the padlock on one of the hatches being unlocked, and through a gap between two tyres Liv caught a glimpse of a starry sky, and she heard her father's voice speaking to her. At last she dared turn on the torch, which she had been clutching in her hand the whole time.

He brought her tea and tinned food, which he had heated on the camping stove outside his workshop. Reaching the stove in the kitchen had become difficult, so now that it was just him doing the cooking he preferred to use his own kitchen, as he called it. He had stretched a canvas sheet over it as an awning, so that it was reasonably protected against the rain. Sometimes he would light one of his home-made torches and stick it in the umbrella stand next to the camping stove. On such occasions, the smell of food and resin would fill the air and Liv imagined that her father was happy.

Right now it was the tea and the food that made Liv happy. The air from the open hatch felt like happiness too. The light was warm and good. Dad was with her.

Liv told him about the darkness and the heavy air. And he left, came back and drilled three holes in the side of the container and metal shavings snowed on the newspaper below. Afterwards he folded the newspaper and placed it and the shavings in between the other newspapers. Then he placed a piece of black fabric over the three holes and fixed it at the top with gaffer tape.

'Now you can have fresh air whenever you want,' he said. 'You'll need to lift up the cloth if you want more air and you can also look out at the road. But be careful with the light. You must never switch on the torch, unless the cloth is in place. The light can be seen from the outside. Do you understand?'

Liv nodded. Then she switched off her torch like a good girl, lifted up the cloth and pressed her face against the three holes arranged as an inverted triangle. Through the bottom hole she took a long, deep breath; she could smell spruces and coarse grass and salty sea air. And through the two top holes she could see the night sky and the moon lighting up the gravel road. Somewhere, an owl was hooting. She imitated it quietly, and smiled when she felt her father's hands on her shoulders.

'You're very good at this,' he whispered. Then he told her that it was best that she stayed in the container until people had finished looking for her. 'The police must be absolutely sure that you're dead, Liv. But then we'll be left in peace.'

She understood. Being left in peace was a good thing.

And one day she was allowed out. Her father lifted her up over the dark blue metal edge and out through the opening with the slanted hatch, even though she insisted she didn't need any help. He had placed a couple of crates and a tractor tyre outside, so she could easily climb back into the container, if necessary. She obviously couldn't lock the hatch from the outside once she was inside, but he had made a device so that she could secure it with a metal bracket from the inside. Just to be on the safe side.

He had a surprise for her in the living room: two baby rabbits that had been left in a box for collection along the roadside. She experienced a strange, unknown joy as she stuck her hand into the cardboard box and stroked the animals' soft fur. They would be allowed to live in the house; they wouldn't be caught in snares in the forest and be flayed and eaten as ragout. The small, living rabbits looked cheerfully at her and chewed and munched and moved about the hay in soft jumps. Liv's heart leapt.

And yet, for some reason, she still began to cry when she climbed into her mother's bed. And for some reason, her mother also cried. Then they ate sweets and biscuits and snapped them and shook them and read a book about a woman who was very much in love. It was Liv who did the reading aloud but her mother who recognized being in love and felt it ripple deep inside her.

★

And one day the child arrived. Too soon. Maria gave birth in the bedroom, which at that point she could just about leave. But only just and only if she forced her way out.

Her husband and daughter helped welcome the baby.

Liv stared at the drama unfolding in front of her eyes. The head. The tiny head that came out towards her like a marbled moon before it became a complete head that stuck out of the bottom of a giant body.

She marvelled at the effort, the fluid, the small body attached to the tiny head which eventually followed it outside, but with great reluctance. A transparent, wet and far too small body with a long, grey-and-white snake squirming from its tummy.

And she heard her mother make noises that grew louder and louder as the hours passed. They weren't screams, not the loud, high-pitched cries of a bird of prey. They were cries that came from deep inside the earth. Deep roars without consonants.

And the earth fought with itself in the bed. The big body lay like a trembling landscape with mountains and gorges and wild shrub fighting in front of Liv.

Shouting.

At something or for something.

And then the tiny person dangling in front of her.
At the head.
And her father holding its feet and slapping it.
Why did he slap it?
And then the silence.
Carl was terrified.

Liv was told to cut the cord with her dagger. They attached a clip. And some gauze. In time she had picked up so many rolls of gauze and compresses and white surgical tape from the small 'help yourself facility' on the outskirts of the Head that a sign had been put up asking the islanders if they really needed quite so much gauze.

The child also fought. It really did. It had fought its way out of the earth, out of the water, out of the darkness, and now it gasped for air, surrounded as it was by so much of it. Without vowels or consonants. It just opened its tiny lips. Like the flounders.

And then it stopped.

It couldn't do it. It was far too small to live.

Liv tried to cover Carl's ears when their father screamed. He screamed like the owl, like the seagulls, like an injured hedgehog; like a deer screams for her lost fawn; like a badger screaming out of passion. He screamed like a child screams when he finds his father dead in the heather.

His scream was as high-pitched as it was possible to scream. A shade of white so blinding and luminous that it was like looking straight at the sun at noon and seeing nothing and everything at once.

But more than anything, Jens Horder screamed as he had screamed on the inside when he discovered his baby boy under the cradle with his skull broken – and at that moment realized the unbearable truth: that in his rush of expectant joy he had forgotten to put in the final screws, that he had failed as a carpenter and a father, that he had killed his own son. And that he would never ever be able to share that truth with his darling wife out of sheer terror of also losing her.

With numb hands he had picked up the side piece and screwed it in place so that no one could tell the two cradles apart. Then he had knelt in front of the lifeless child on the floor. He hadn't touched it; he had stared at the small head in the scarlet halo and finally screamed at the top of his lungs until Maria had come running and picked up the child and held it tight and screamed in unison with him.

The back of Carl's soft head had hit one of his father's toolboxes as he fell. A merciless, steel-grey corner.

That was how Jens screamed now. And Liv recognized her father's scream from an early memory.

Maria cried herself to sleep with soft vowels, and Liv washed her bloodstained mother while her father disappeared with the small, lifeless body.

'It was a girl,' was all he said as he walked away with the child in his arms.

*Dear Liv*

*We should never have tried to give you a baby sister or brother, but your dad insisted. We must have two, he said. Just like before. Just like he had had a brother, and you should have had a twin brother. We would restore the balance, he said, and after all, I loved him. I still do.*

*But perhaps that child was never intended to live because we wouldn't have been able to look after it, not properly. I was scared of giving birth to it. Scared of giving birth to it far too soon and scared that it would be alive when it got out of me. I was frightened of the child. Frightened for the child.*

*So I didn't press it out as I should have; I tried to keep it inside me. I squashed it; perhaps it suffocated. Perhaps I killed my own child.*

*Or perhaps some children aren't meant to live. Perhaps your baby sister wasn't meant to live, and perhaps it isn't my fault.*

*I don't know, Liv.*

*I've also tried to come to terms with Carl's accident, but I've failed. I suspected your granny because she was on medication, which made her unpredictable at times. It mostly made her drowsy, but she could also suddenly become irascible, wild. It frightened me, and deep down I think it frightened her as well.*

*Carl cried a great deal, and perhaps she couldn't handle it. That's what we think happened. She couldn't handle his crying, and so she took him from the cradle, shook him, and dropped him on the toolbox on the floor. Perhaps she did it on purpose? We think so. That's why it was a relief when she moved. And yet I cannot find peace because I will never know what really happened.*

*Perhaps it wasn't her at all. What if it was me? I got so little sleep the days blurred into one another, and I too was sick in my own way, in my head. Exhausted and frightened for the future. At times I couldn't remember what I had just done. Might I have hurt your twin brother?*

*If I had, could you forgive me?*

All my love,
Mum

# The Pub and the Child

When a brutal storm grabs a big chunk of coastline, people notice. Men with pipes and briefcases tucked under their arms stand in far too smart shoes for the harsh landscape, narrowing their eyes before taking measurements with too long strides in the morning fog and making notes about the direction of the wind and the risk of mudslide on lined notepads with blue ballpoint pens before they drive back and drink coffee. But when a peaceful sea decides to lick its way quietly through a headland, no one pays attention, at least not to begin with. Who would notice if a little sand disappears on each side? How the sea intrudes inconspicuously, adding inch after inch to itself.

The Neck grew a little slimmer every year, but only a little. The gravel road's parallel universes of seaweed and stones and sand and box thorn diminished proportionally, but unobserved. And the gravel road itself was being suffocated by weeds that lived in very little danger of being flattened by cars. The most frequent traffic these days was a solitary child running off at night with an empty rucksack, only to return home with a full one.

★

Roald scratched his head as he studied the contents of the fridge. He was pretty sure there had been two foil trays of

Dauphinoise potatoes rather than just one. He was also fairly sure that he had put a bottle of fizzy lemon pop near the front of the shelf before going to bed. He looked about him. There were no other signs to indicate that someone had been in the pub kitchen.

His initial conclusion was that one of the guests must have sneaked down to the kitchen and helped himself to a late-night snack. But it still didn't add up. This had become a regular occurrence, every few days at times, and in between he would notice that things other than food had gone missing. Odd things. One morning he had searched in vain for a deck of cards he was certain he had left on the kitchen table the night before; another time, the chef discovered that a saucepan was missing. By now there had been countless incidents, all of which defied explanation.

Now, the chef himself might be the culprit, but it seemed highly unlikely. He simply wasn't like that. Roald couldn't think of a more trustworthy man than his culinary-skilled distant cousin, and he refused to believe that the man would jeopardize his trusted position through impulsive and insignificant petty thefts.

Besides, the chef reacted with total composure whenever he discovered that something was missing. He simply laughed it off. He laughed everything off. Then again, to claim that he was in complete control of his kitchen and the items in the stock room would be something of an exaggeration. In fact, the chef probably suspected Roald of sneaking down at night to scoff the leftovers. When he hinted at this with a glint in his eye, Roald would protest vociferously, but he couldn't help laughing too, and that was always the end of that.

But then who could it be? Who on earth would want to help themselves to leftovers and decks of cards and ballpoint pens and fizzy pop and tinned tuna from the stock room? And how did they do it?

That night there had been no guests staying over at the pub so the possibility that the thief might be a guest was now completely eliminated.

Roald left the kitchen and walked down the short back stairs to the small corridor that led to the stock room. It took him some time to realize that some rolls of kitchen towel, a few packets of crispbread and crackers, several tins of tomatoes, some sausages, possibly a jar of honey and definitely a large bag of biscuits . . . and some bubble wrap were missing. Yes, there had definitely been a lot of bubble wrap in the big cardboard box in which the new trouser press had been delivered. And now it was gone.

Bubble wrap? Who would nick that? The gloves that Roald wore whenever he handled frozen goods were also gone.

As he walked back through the corridor he stopped for a moment and looked up at the small, rectangular basement window, which as usual was ajar, because fresh air was good for you. But surely no one could get in through that window. It was impossible.

The kitchen was closed for the next fortnight because, for the first time in twenty years, the chef had decided to take a proper holiday. He and his wife were taking a trip to the mainland but might return sooner than planned if they didn't enjoy being away.

Given that the public bar and several of the first-floor guest rooms were in need of painting and various minor repairs, Roald decided to deal with that at the same time and pretty much close the pub in the meantime. He could carry out the work himself, thank God, which would bring the cost down. If he did find himself in need of help after all, he knew who to ask: the regulars were keen to return to their watering hole and were willing to don a boiler suit, if that was what it took. Especially if it also involved beer. Roald, however, had initially turned them down because he wanted some time to himself.

He made a quick decision. He took out a bag of flour and left it in the kitchen. Before he went to bed that night he would sprinkle a very fine layer across the floor. He could always sweep it up the next day. He intended to do this for the next few nights now that he knew that he was the only one going into the kitchen. Never mind the hassle of sweeping it up, Roald needed to know what was going on.

To add to the fun, he left a broken pencil, six liquorice pastilles and a deck of cards on the table. And he put exactly twenty-five slices of salami on a plate in the fridge, as well as ten slices of ham and five rings of red pepper.

The first five mornings he inspected the kitchen there were no signs of anything amiss. The sixth morning the pencil was gone, as were three of the pastilles, seven slices of salami, two slices of ham and one ring of red pepper. And there were footprints in the flour between the fridge and the kitchen table and the door to the basement corridor. Roald squatted down on his haunches and stared, baffled, at the clearest of the prints. It was very small. It had to be a child.

When he followed the footprints out into the corridor and below the window, the penny dropped. With a little bit of ingenuity, a child might be able to get in and out that way.

But a child? At night?

And why steal bubble wrap?

While Roald was repairing a strip of flooring in a first-floor guest room, his thoughts circled around the night-time visits. He wished more than anything that he could dismiss them as an innocent childish prank, but it was impossible. A child who regularly stole food and flour and saucepans and kitchen towels must be a child in need.

However, there were no children in need in Korsted. Judging by the size of the shoeprint, it was a young child. A boy, he imagined, without questioning why he thought so.

Roald wouldn't claim to know every child in town, yet he knew quite a few and thought he had a fair idea of who they were and where they lived. Not one of them fitted the narrative playing out in the pub kitchen in any way. The baker's three boys were fond of making mischief, but they couldn't possibly be behind the break-ins. Roald's reasoning was partly that he didn't think any of them would be able to squeeze through the narrow window but, more importantly, he was convinced that they would have woken up everyone in the pub before they even reached the back of the house. The boys were much noisier than other people's children. Even when they played sleeping lions, you had to press your hands over your ears. Whenever Roald encountered the three boys and the volume of the noise they made, he was overcome by spontaneous gratitude at being childless. He pitied the sixth-form teacher who would one day do battle with their hormones.

On the other hand, Roald's heart nearly exploded with joy whenever he saw the police officer's daughter. She was the loveliest, tiniest human being he knew. Always wore a dress and had her hair in plaits, as if she lived in a Little House on the Prairie, rather than a large, yellow-brick house in the middle of the high street. And her name was Laura; it was almost too good to be true. But apart from Roald's heart, little Laura was unlikely ever to have stolen anything.

So who could it be? He went through the children one by one, and he couldn't imagine any one of them sneaking out at night to go scavenging for food. Everyone had what they needed, as far as he was aware. And if they brought home stolen goods, surely their parents would start noticing eventually, for goodness' sake.

Roald had always been very careful not to spread rumours in the public bar, and for that reason he had kept his knowledge of the thefts to himself. On one occasion he had asked some of the regulars in a roundabout way if there were people on the island suffering actual hardship, people who found it difficult to make ends meet.

The regulars had scratched their heads and suggested a slightly down-at-heel old woman with a pram who often

wandered around the junkyard. And then there was the village idiot from the derelict farm with the Shetland ponies.
And the three drunkards who lived in a lean-to near the
ferry berth, or at least they had done so recently.

However, the regulars had soon agreed that none of
these people were in dire need. The drunkards looked like
they had enough to drink, the village idiot had enough to
eat – at least, considerably more than his poor ponies. And
it was believed that the old lady with the pram lived in a
nice thatched cottage on the road to Sønderby – with a
neatly trimmed box hedge and a fine little windmill in her
front garden. Her husband was a retired bookkeeper. She
was just crazy.

And then there was Jens Horder on the Head; now he
had always been a bit odd and difficult to get close to. He
drove around with a lot of junk, but that didn't necessarily
equal hardship, and he certainly had plenty of stuff at
home. Nor was his wife thought to suffer serious hardship
because, according to the postman, she had grown quite
big. By the way, it was a very long time since anyone had
seen her south of the Head.

Horder had a child, Roald remembered. *Had.* Everyone on the island knew that the poor girl had died at sea.
Imagine being a parent struck by such a tragedy. It didn't
make it any less tragic that a few years earlier they had lost
a baby, also in an accident. As far as Roald had gathered,
it had been the girl's twin brother. How cruel is fate
allowed to be? So if you weren't already a little odd, surely
such experiences would make you so.

Roald remembered the sound of the helicopter restlessly

criss-crossing the island and the shoreline during the search for the girl. If only they had found a body.

You would surely reach that point eventually. Wanting to find the body. At some stage, hope would die like a tired fire and become a small, glowing wish. It was better than nothing.

Imagine getting to that point.

The strip of flooring was in place, and he shifted back slightly to look at it. At least that wasn't going anywhere.

So it couldn't be Horder's child, either. For obvious reasons.

Could it be a dwarf?

He dismissed the thought and got up. If a hungry dwarf with a penchant for bubble wrap lived somewhere on the island, he would undoubtedly have heard about it.

He needed a beer.

Roald flopped into the office chair and stared at the telephone. The curved black handle lay neatly across the cradle. The glossy Bakelite had grown a little dull from being held by sweaty hands, and the once so transparent dial had taken on a taupe hue of dust and dirt. Roald took a swig of his beer.

He knew that he ought to contact the police. He had built up an excellent relationship with the police officer, who was a sympathetic man, when you could get him off duty.

But still he hesitated. Why?

After the next gulp he had made up his mind. He wiped the froth off his lips and set the empty bottle down on the table. He would start by trying to get to the bottom of this himself. There was no need to make a big drama out of it, and the police officer wasn't going anywhere.

There had always been a few days between the night-time visits, so Roald waited four days. On the fifth evening he went to bed early and caught a few hours of shut-eye before getting up around midnight. Then he tiptoed down to the kitchen and began his vigil. He had set out various items and had even fetched a pile of Donald Duck comics from the bookcase on the landing. On the rare occasions that children were among the pub's visitors, the comics were usually a hit. Now they were laid out on the kitchen table.

If only he had been able to turn on the light, then he would have been able to read a book, or a Donald Duck comic, for that matter, but it was out of the question. Any kind of light would be seen through the windows. At one point he fell asleep, slumped across the small table where he was sitting, and around five in the morning he was woken up by pins and needles in his arm. The house was as quiet as the grave, and he tiptoed back upstairs to bed.

Another few nights passed in a similar fashion: no visits. And then, finally, on Monday night something happened. This time Roald had brewed himself a cup of strong coffee in the hope that it would keep him up until the early morning, and at two thirty he was still wide awake. His mind was focused and his thoughts moved calmly back and forth between tax accounts, whisky stocks, ex-colleagues and his ex-wife to pest control and pools football. He was even enjoying sitting here, thinking, while everyone else was asleep. Outside, the wind was blowing just enough for the pub sign to squeak on its hinges, and a branch from a bush scratched the wall softly.

And then suddenly another sound came from the back of the building. It was quite faint, but it was there. He got up as quietly as he could and retreated to his hiding place in the corner, next to the dining room. He was able to squeeze in next to a tall cupboard and stand unnoticed in the darkness.

Soon he heard the handle on the door to the corridor being pushed slowly down. It wasn't in his field of vision. But the fridge was. And soon the boy was too.

Roald held his breath as he saw the small figure approach the fridge. If it hadn't been for his eyes adjusting to the darkness over the previous few hours, he wouldn't have been able to see a thing, but now he could clearly see the contours of a small boy. Shortish hair, slim build, and holding a large bag, possibly a rucksack, in his hand. He moved with impressive lightness and didn't make a sound. Roald couldn't hear a single one of his footsteps.

The boy didn't turn on the light, but he evidently knew his way to the fridge. He opened the fridge door, only very slightly, but enough to see what it contained. As he had his back to Roald, his face wasn't revealed by the fridge light, but Roald had time to catch sight of dark, straggly hair and a brown-and-orange-striped sweater. The next moment, the boy took out a foil tray and closed the fridge door. He stayed where he was, sniffing the tray, which contained the leftovers of the meal Roald had cooked for himself the night before. Spaghetti Bolognese. It wasn't at all bad.

The boy ate a little with his fingers before putting the foil tray back, quickly and noiselessly, apart from the hissing sound which the door made when the rubber strips found one another again. Then he licked his fingers clean and turned to the table where Roald had been sitting. His hand reached the Donald Duck comics and, for a brief second, a tiny beam of light revealed Scrooge McDuck's face. Then it was dark again. The boy put his rucksack on the table, took some magazines from the bottom of the pile and put them in his bag. Then his hand sought out the small glass bowl with sweets, and there was a momentary flash of multiple colours. He grabbed a handful and let liquorice pastilles and gummy bears trickle into a side pocket of his rucksack. A single pastille missed; it hit the floor with a small ping and rattled over the floor tiles.

The boy stood stock-still and listened out while he waited. Roald did likewise. No noise came from the rest of the house. Then the boy bent down, felt with his hands across the floor until he found the pastille and popped it into his mouth.

Was he going to take anything else? Continue to the stock room? Roald didn't want to reveal himself yet. To his amazement, he was not only intrigued but also overcome with a strange tenderness towards his shy guest. There was something infinitely tragic about how skilled the boy was at executing his routine. Roald felt no anger at all, only compassion. And wonder.

The boy began exploring drawers and cupboards with

great caution. At times the small cone of light would strike something, but only ever as a flash. Something was fished out of a drawer and put in the rucksack. Roald tried guessing what it might be. A hand whisk, possibly. The boy also took a pair of oven mitts, or possibly just the one. Then he suddenly hoisted up the rucksack and went back to the door.

Roald hesitated. Was now the time to make himself known? Should he step forward, clear his throat? The boy would probably get the shock of his life if he did. Perhaps he had better wait until the kid was on his way out of the window? Why the hell hadn't he made a plan of his own?

The boy disappeared out of Roald's field of vision. A faint squeak revealed that the door had been opened and closed. Soon afterwards there was a barely audible sound from the corridor; it came from the door to the stock room. If Roald hadn't been expecting the sound, he would never have heard it. It might easily have been the wind. For a moment he hesitated in his hideout next to the cupboard, trying to collect his thoughts.

Finally he came forward. He didn't head for the door to the corridor, although he knew that his stock room was in the process of being raided. He slipped out of another door – through the living room, out into the hall, out through the front door. He moved more silently than he had ever done, and thanked the wind for being a little noisier now. When he had closed the heavy front door carefully behind him, he turned to the small reception area in front of the pub. In one of the flower beds a couple of large bushes were swaying in the glow from the street-light. Apart from that, everything was quiet.

The road to the north was just as deserted as the reception area. At that time of night any human activity would have been strange. Roald walked softly along the front of the pub until he reached the corner, from where he had a view of the driveway round to the back and thus the open basement window. The light from the nearest street lamp didn't reach this far, but a crescent moon threw a faint glow over the gravel and the pub.

The first item to appear might well be toilet paper. An economy pack of twelve, which you could just about squeeze through the window frame. Afterwards, followed . . . a roll of some sort? Maybe oilcloth. Then the rucksack. Two skinny arms in a stripy jumper arranged everything outside to make room.

And then the child followed.

After he had climbed out, the boy left the window ajar, as he had found it. Then he put on the rucksack, picked up the toilet paper and the oilcloth and moved almost silently across the gravel and out on to the tarmac road. Roald stared after him. He still couldn't decide whether to make himself known to the boy.

So instead he followed him. In the shadows.

The boy didn't run, not really, but neither did he walk. There was something floating about his gait. Roald was reminded of indigenous people and Asian field workers who carried heavy loads over long distances.

However, what puzzled Roald wasn't so much the gait. It was the direction. The child was following the road northwards. Did he live in one of the houses scattered along the road a little further up? Were there even children his age living there?

There were few streetlights north of Korsted. Roald hesitated momentarily at the prospect of moving in the dark. But the moon hung like a golden sabre, reflecting the rays of a distant sun. There was light, a little light. Enough for him to see the small figure ahead of him. But what if the boy saw him? He really didn't want to frighten the child.

It was a great stroke of luck for Roald that the road was winding and flanked by different types of shrubs. It gave him the chance to move faster when he was under cover and in no danger of being seen; he was forced to admit that he was unable to move at the same speed as the child. The boy had to be as strong as an ox.

After some time the landscape opened up again and further ahead, where the road passed a small cluster of houses, there were streetlights, but only a few. The boy, however, seemed to want to evade the light because he veered off across the field and ran left around the houses. Halfway across the field, Roald had to stop. Panting, he stared after the small figure that had disappeared into the darkness to the north.

Was the boy really heading out to the Head?

*Dear Liv*

*The other day you were about to say something about some traps – when you suddenly stopped. You wouldn't say anything more. You've got me worried.*

   *What kind of traps?*
   *What are you not telling me?*
   *I wish you were here now.*
   *I wish you were here to keep me company. I miss you.*

*Love,*
*Mum*

# Retention

Jens Horder carried the newborn baby outside. Outside the shrinking bedroom, along the narrow corridor, down the stairs that contracted with each step, through the rooms of the house, which dwindled to dusty airways. And he went out into the yard, where the sky tried to penetrate the forest of indispensable junk, but found the ground only when small passages criss-crossed the heaps like rabbit tracks in the grass. He reached his workshop and placed his newborn daughter on the workbench on the small quilted blanket in which he had carried her. She was a child who didn't scream.

Jens Horder didn't scream either, not any more. He was calm now, focused.

When Liv joined him, he had finished washing the child. Without asking questions, she carried the basin of water outside and emptied it behind the workshop, as he had asked her to. And she filled it again with water from the pump. For his hands, he had said. And she found the oils in the kitchen for him. And the empty jam jars. And she fetched the bags of gauze. And she helped him with the sack of salt. And she lit the camping stove outside and started cleaning the resin, as he had taught her. They would need it later, he said. Except for the jam jars and the salt; they were for now. She couldn't see Carl anywhere.

Liv tried to stay calm, but she was scared and confused. And in that moment she was acutely aware that she was only a child.

Jens fetched a kitchen knife and held it over the flame while Liv sat next to him. She wanted to ask him, but couldn't. She opened her mouth, but no air came in and no sounds came out. Then she followed him back inside the workshop. He walked as if he didn't know that she was there; as if he didn't see her. As if she were Carl.

Liv could see the edge of the quilted blanket hanging crookedly over the corner of the workbench, and she could see two bare feet which were so tiny, much smaller than hers. An oil lamp beside them caused the feet to cast woolly shadows. Only they didn't look warm.

Carl had yet to turn up, and Liv didn't know whether to stay or go. Her father was standing by the workbench and she could hear him breathe. The tiny toes lay very still. She walked closer, positioned herself on the other side of the workbench and looked up at him. He didn't see her. He was looking down at the blanket.

Recently, his breathing had changed, as if there were wood shavings in the air he inhaled. Sometimes she wanted to help him breathe, breathe in unison with him or maybe breathe in while he breathed out. And at times she wanted to drag him out into the forest. They hadn't been there for a long time now. The air in the forest was nicer than in the workshop . . . and far better than in the house and the container. She missed the forest.

And now she didn't know what to do.

When she couldn't make up her mind, her body made it for her. She slumped on to the floor behind the workbench in a gliding movement, as if falling into herself.

Then she rested her chin on the workbench crossbeam. The empty jam jars were in front of her on the sawdust on the floor. And so were her father's legs. He had a hole in one trouser leg, a tear just below his knee, and she imagined his skin behind the hole. Would she be able to see it if she shone a torch at it? The beam from her tiny torch hit the hole and the skin, which looked like parched soil. It was full of small, thirsty wrinkles, and she wanted to touch it.

Suddenly the knees came towards her. A knee popped out of the tear, and she could see it clearly in the torchlight. It looked like a baby's head coming out of its mum. Then her father's hand reached down for a jam jar; he picked it up like a hook gripping it under water. And she heard his breath with wood shavings in it, and a sound like a knife going into a rabbit. And shortly afterwards the jam jar was lowered down on to the sawdust. Now it contained something dark. And his hand left dark imprints on the glass. Another jar was picked up and disappeared over the edge of the workbench, only to return with something in it. And so it went on. She stared at the full jars and remembered the rabbits and the stags. And she shone the torch at one of them and recognized what she was looking at.

At that moment Carl was back with her and took her hand.

She whispered for him not to be afraid. It was just their baby sister's lungs in a jam jar.

*

Then her father came. No, first his knee moved forwards, then his upper body bent down, then one hand held on to the edge, then his head, which was tilted slightly, and with his head came his eyes looking at her over the crossbeam under the workbench. She switched off her torch.

'What are you doing?' he asked her quietly. His voice had changed. Perhaps his voice also had wood shavings in it now.

She could hear something drip from the workbench. At first several drops, then the intervals between them grew shorter before they turned into one sound, a spray.

'Waiting, I think,' Liv replied. 'What are you doing?'

He sat very still. Just as still as Carl. Suddenly the spray became drops once more.

'I'm getting your baby sister ready. So that we can take good care of her.'

'OK.'

'I think you should help.'

'OK.'

'Please would you stand up?'

'Yes.'

Liv tried to stand up, but Carl refused. He pushed her down on to the floor as if she were a heavy sack of salt.

Her father became trouser legs once more.

'So are you coming, Liv?' he said from somewhere above her.

'Yes,' she said, without moving.

'There's nothing to be scared of,' he said.

'OK.'

Carl released his grip, and she stood up with his hand in hers. Together they held their breath.

★

Jens Horder didn't remember the details; perhaps he had never known them. But preserved inside him were the outlines of knowledge, a rough skeleton of insight into the methods of ages past into which his father had once initiated him. And it was this knowledge which now guided his hands.

He didn't want to preserve his newborn daughter in order to save her soul. He just wanted to preserve his daughter. To keep her.

Not have to lose her.

The small body was cleaned thoroughly on the inside and the organs removed so only the heart remained. It had to be there, he remembered, and it felt right. She was the most beautiful little girl. Just as beautiful as his Liv had once been.

And her twin brother.

He had to preserve this fragile human being so that she wouldn't disappear into the ground, as his son had done seven years ago. He could no longer hold on to Carl in pencil sketches. The lines couldn't retain the flesh; the perspective couldn't embrace his shape. Carl was slowly being erased from the very same memory that so desperately tried to keep him there. And Jens Horder refused to lose yet another much wanted and loved child.

Jens Horder refused to lose anything ever again.

Something inside him told him that Liv had to be

there. Liv's presence was necessary to keep the dead new-born present.

The salt would extract all moisture from the body, her father explained while he looked for a basin the right size. Liv had never seen so much salt at once. She looked at the small face as the white sea rose around her baby sister. The small eyes were closed. Carl had also closed his and Liv would have liked to, but she couldn't. She was supposed to help her father. She had to be a part of everything; he had asked her to. Together they would look after the little girl and make sure that she didn't disappear.

Except that right now she was disappearing in a bath of salt, and her cheeks and her tiny nose were the last things to drown.

She would need to lie in the basin for a month until she had dried up completely, until there wasn't a single drop of moisture left in her, he had said. Liv wondered whether you could cry when you were dead.

Carl certainly could. In fact, he had started to cry a great deal. He cried because their baby sister was dead, and he cried because their mum was upstairs in the bedroom and mustn't know anything about the child in the salt, and he cried because their dad had started acting so strangely. He cried because they had to hide in the container whenever there was the slightest suspicion that someone was coming. Yes, even if they heard the tiniest sound. And perhaps he cried the hardest because he felt very alone, even when he was with Liv.

Maria Horder hadn't had the strength to bury yet another child, and she had nodded gratefully from her overburdened bed when Jens came upstairs to tell her that the newborn had been burned and was gone. He had built a fine, tiny coffin for her in which she had gone on her way, he had said. Then he had kissed his wife's forehead and stroked her hair.

'She's all right,' he had whispered.

And Liv had listened from her mother's bedside. She didn't feel good. She knew that this was one of the times it was OK to lie. When you *had* to lie. She must never tell her mum that the little person who had come out of her hadn't been burned but was buried in a basin of salt in the workshop. She must never tell her, never ever.

So Liv said nothing; instead, she read aloud to her mother. She had become incredibly good at it, Maria said, whenever she was able to get a sound past her soft lips. Usually she would grab one of her many notebooks and write something for Liv, who lunged at the sentences like a starving child.

*I'm so proud that you know how to read and write so well already. It's really wonderful, Liv.*

And Liv smiled, sated with happiness for a moment before she read on.

Aloud.

From time to time she wondered whether she couldn't just write down her secret and show it to Mum. In that way she wouldn't actually have said anything but she would rid herself of her knowledge. Without having spoken a word.

But she didn't dare. It was no longer just strangers who frightened her. Her father's increasing moroseness was creeping up on her like a dark and ominous threat.

Maria Horder no longer left the bedroom. But even if she had been capable of doing so during the month her lifeless third child lay buried in salt, she wouldn't have recognized her own home any more. She, too, was slowly being buried.

*Dear Liv*

*The rabbits – what's happening to the rabbits? Have we got more of them? I think I can hear them. Don't they live in their hutch any more? And the animals in the barn . . . I can also hear the animals. Don't you feed them?*

*It's night-time now. They shouldn't be making any noise.*

*Love,*
*Mum*

# My Baby Sister

While my baby sister dried out in the salt, I collected more gauze and cleaned more resin and Mum wondered at the smell that lingered about me. *You smell of resin, you must be out in the forest a lot*, she wrote. And I whispered: 'It's a scent, not a smell.'

Then she smiled.

One night I found a big sack of stale pastries behind the bakery, and we spent a lot of time enjoying them in bed. Carl got a little worried that Mum ate so many, at which point I sent him outside. He really could be a pain sometimes. Dad didn't want any, and that made me a bit sad because I liked it best when we were together, the three of us. These days we hardly ever were.

But what was worse was that he was starting to lose his temper. Not with me, not directly, and not with Mum either. He always spoke nicely to us – when he did speak, that is. So I don't really know who he was angry with, but at times I would hear him rant and rave when he was all on his own. Perhaps he too had an invisible friend to shout at.

Every now and then I would shout a little at Carl, but never enough to make him disappear from me . . . become a completely invisible twin brother, I mean.

And other things began to worry me. There really was

a lot of stuff everywhere and although I liked all of it, especially the things Dad and I had found together, something felt wrong.

I would compare our house with those I visited, houses where it was much easier for me to move about the rooms. They weren't quite so dusty and dirty either. And although the mice and the spiders were my friends, it was nice that there were no mouse droppings and cobwebs in the pub kitchen. The other houses seemed so different, and they smelled different too. They had a scent. Especially the pub.

I was old enough to remember that we hadn't always had as many things as we did now. That we had once been able to use the kitchen and bathroom for their proper purposes, rather than just to store things in.

I think I would have liked it to have stayed that way. Not to have quite so many things. On the other hand, I didn't want to be without any of the things we had. And Dad had said that we had to look after them.

So this was all weighing on my mind, only I didn't know what to do about it. I found it harder and harder to talk to Dad, and I was scared of saying anything to Mum that might make her sad – or worse. Whenever I wanted to tell her something that I strongly suspected Dad wouldn't want me to, I could hear his voice in my head saying: *It would kill your mum.*

Now, I had killed animals, and I was even quite good at it. But I desperately didn't want to kill my mum.

I couldn't imagine anything worse than her not lying upstairs in her bed, waiting for me. Waiting for me to bring her more food and a book to read to her while she stroked my hair and mimed that she loved me. These days it was my favourite thing, now that Dad no longer took me out in the dinghy or even into the forest. Ever since my baby sister had come out of Mum, he rarely went anywhere.

It's hard to talk to someone when you can't say what you want. Especially when the person you're talking to doesn't say very much, whether they're your mum or your dad or your invisible twin brother. I think that's why I loved reading aloud to Mum so much.

That way I could be sure that I still could. Speak, I mean.

But I still wasn't allowed to mention certain things. And outside the bedroom I was expected to be quiet the whole time so that no one would hear me.

So it seemed odd that Dad sent me down to the main island alone, given how scared he was that someone might see me. He said the same thing every time: *For God's sake, don't let anyone see you. And don't tell your mum that I'm not with you.*

I didn't understand why God, who we didn't believe in anyway, kept getting mixed up in everything. And it made even less sense that Dad stayed at home and looked after the things rather than coming with me so he could watch out for *me*. I didn't work out until later that he was even more scared than I was. Of all sorts of things, I think. A little bit like Carl.

And there was another thing I had started to wonder about. Carl had started to feel pain at night, in the darkness. When we walked home across the Neck and our feet got blisters. Or on the night we burned our hands on a wood-burning stove in someone's living room. Or the night we bumped into an old steel sink someone had leaned against a wall.

Carl had really hurt himself. And I had bled. And perhaps I had hurt myself a bit too.

I was starting to think that the darkness probably couldn't hold much more pain, and so the pain had to stay inside Carl and in me. The darkness was full to bursting with pain. Just like our house.

Perhaps Dad could feel it too. Perhaps he was also hurting in the dark. But perhaps he didn't think that I was. And I didn't know how to tell him.

★

The body that came out of the salt was totally different to the one I saw disappear into it. My baby sister, who was very small to start with, had grown even smaller. She was so thin, so thin. But perhaps that was what happened to you if you didn't eat for a month? I wondered whether the same thing might happen to Mum, if she tried it.

Dad put her on the workbench again. It was still very dark from the blood that had run out of her last time – through the quilted blanket and into the wood. There was also a big dark stain on the floor. Now there wasn't a drop left in her; exactly as he had hoped.

We needed the oils and the resin now. My job was to melt clean resin on the camping stove outside the workshop. I used the saucepan from the pub. The resin must be liquid, Dad said. Not boiling, just liquid. When I came inside with my first batch he had smeared my baby sister in oil. One of the big bottles of grapeseed oil was almost empty, and she lay glossy on the workbench.

I thought it was nice that there was no more blood and that he had closed up the hole in her stomach. He took the saucepan from me and poured liquid resin all over her, and afterwards he spread it with a brush, making sure to cover everything.

He did it very carefully, just like when he drew, and although she was very small and skinny she suddenly looked quite beautiful as she lay there. My baby sister. I so wished that she wasn't dead.

He had put out a stool for me so I would have a better view of everything. It was strange because, in one way, I wanted to run away – to run upstairs and hide in the bedroom with Mum or outside to hide in the container with Carl.

In another way, I wanted to stay on the stool and watch everything. Be there with Dad.

It was just as well that I was there because he really needed me now. My, oh my, did we use a lot of gauze. I handed him one roll after another and he wrapped my baby sister in it. He started with her tiny feet and continued all the way up over her tiny head so her whole face disappeared under narrow strips of thin fabric. No air must get to the skin, he explained.

When she was finally swaddled from head to foot I thought that we had finished. But no. He just poured more resin over her, and then it was back to the gauze.

And so we carried on until Dad finally said that he thought it was enough.

And then he did something that took me completely by surprise. He fetched a drawing. A new drawing. And this although it was a long time since I'd seen him draw anything at all. This one was different from his other drawings because it was made with black ink on a thin wooden sheet. He held it up so that I could see it. 'Do you think it looks like her?' he asked.

I didn't, as it happens, seeing as she had grown so skinny and was now wrapped in all sorts of things. But it looked like her right before she drowned in salt.

I nodded.

'We'll place it on top of her face, so we can always remember what she looks like inside.'

Dad put the drawing in place and attached it with more gauze along the sides. Then he took a big piece of canvas and wrapped it around her. It was quite incredible how much she was wrapped up. He also cut an oval hole in the canvas over her head so that you could see the drawing.

Now my baby sister looked like one of those wooden dolls that fit one inside another. We had once found some in a living room in Vesterby. Only ours was bigger and there was only one little girl inside.

Finally she was placed in the tiny coffin Dad had made for her. I had heard him sawing and hammering and planing and sanding while I was sitting in the container.

I had started spending a lot of time in the container, even if there was no sign of strangers turning up. Come to think of it, no strangers ever called these days, except for the postman, who would pull up by the barrier and get out of his car to put our letters in the post box. I was, of course, extra careful about hiding around the time when he usually called. I could see him through the holes. Even though he was far away – so far away that he was only a small man dressed in red – I was sure that he looked up at the house and at the three small holes in the container every time. I always held my breath and sat as quiet as a mouse until he had driven off again.

But even when the postman had been and gone, Dad would still whisper for me to be careful. The postman might come back, he said. Or other people might spot me and take me away.

In time he only made a sound – a *hiiiiish* – which meant I had to hide quickly.

I guess I could have stayed with Mum in the bedroom. I would probably have been able to find a place to hide or made one for myself, if I moved some stuff around. But the container was better, Dad said, because no one would ever think to look there. I got the impression that he would rather I wasn't with Mum, and I couldn't understand why.

Perhaps he was scared that I might let something slip.

In the end it was easier just to stay in the container with Carl and look out of the holes towards the gravel road. I could tell Carl everything, but he didn't stroke my hair like Mum, and I couldn't really cuddle him. Luckily, I had found a big brown teddy bear in a box. It was a little scruffy, but nice to touch. I could cuddle that.

Whenever I needed to touch something that touched me back I would take one of the rabbits from the house with me into the container. The rabbit felt soft and warm when it moved under my hand, and the feeling gave me sunshine in my tummy. And yet I was terrified. Terrified that Dad might notice, because he had told me that the rabbits must stay in the house. They might make a noise in the container.

When I sat in the darkness, looking out of the holes, I would get very scared at the thought of anyone coming. And yet whenever a movement down by the gravel road turned out to be a rabbit or a fox and not another human being, I got a little bit disappointed. I couldn't understand why.

I also kept an eye on the trees. The area between the forest and the gravel road had always been grassy, but recently a lot of small spruces had started shooting up. It was as if the forest was spreading. Perhaps it might cover all of the Head one day. And I would be safe in the container, right in the middle of it all.

She should be with me, Dad said, when he had finished my baby sister's coffin.

So that we could keep one another company.

We pushed aside some of the old tyres and shifted some sacks so that she could lie in her coffin next to my spot in the container. If I removed the wooden lid, I could look down at her.

The coffin was the nicest thing I had ever seen Dad make. Mum had told me about Grandad's famous coffins, but they couldn't possibly have been more beautiful than the one Dad made for my baby sister.

To begin with, it was a bit odd, her lying there next to me. But in time I grew used to it. Somehow it was nice that we were together, all three of us: my twin brother, our baby sister and me. All of us dead.

Except that I was only reported dead.

*Dear Liv*

*What day is it today? Have you had your birthday? It's so dark here in the bedroom. I wish I could get your dad to move some of the things blocking the windows, but he doesn't come here very often these days. Perhaps you can reach the stuff at the top, if you stand on something? Only I don't want you to get hurt. You might easily get hurt by that big radio at the top.*

*Oh, Liv, you're gone for so long every time. I wish I could get out of bed, out of this room, downstairs. Outside. Please bring the bucket and the flannel soon. And more food and something to drink. I'm so terribly thirsty. It's the air.*

*Mum*

# Northbound

The chef would be back in a few days and the pub would reopen. Roald had finished painting and carried out the repairs, and was now looking forward to the aroma of the chef's delicious food replacing the smell of paint. He had finished a day early but felt strangely restless. It was probably just another loose end which he could tie up, although he had completed every job on his list. He believed that he had earned his first day off in — what was it now? Six, seven, eight years? He had totally lost any sense of time.

Island time was different to mainland time. Back there, he had seen a clear, straight line on his retina whenever he imagined the passing of the year: a linear path with razor-sharp divisions into end-of-year exams, study leave, holidays and meetings; it was always a copy of the equally fixed routines of previous years and next year's invariable plans. On the island, a year was an organic entity that wrapped itself softly around Christmas and stretched out in the summer, where it merged with the years before and after. Time hadn't been suspended; it had just acquired a new velocity. It had become a soft friend that wanted nothing but to be.

Although he had enjoyed the silence while the pub was closed, Roald had to admit that he missed his regulars turning up at the usual time in the bar. He was almost at the stage where he missed the fishcake wholesaler who spent all his visits in front of the one-armed bandit, until the time was exactly eleven minutes to dinner time. It took the fishcake wholesaler nine and a half minutes from leaving his barstool in front of the fruit machine to him leaning his bike up against the wall of his house, he had explained. And then ninety seconds from parking the bike to reaching his dining chair, if he stopped off to wash his hands first.

That was pretty much all the talking the fishcake wholesaler ever did.

Except for stating that crispy pork with parsley sauce should be declared a national dish. Especially if that was what he would be getting for dinner once he got back. On such occasions he could barely suppress his excitement and came very close to leaving his barstool at twelve minutes to. He didn't care much for fishcakes, he said, but it had been a good business right until the reds turned up and wrecked everything with all their ideas. Roald never got to the bottom of what that meant. Nor was he terribly up to speed with the fishcake market.

Roald had yet to discuss the child with anyone. He had bumped into the police officer a few times recently, so it wasn't for lack of opportunity, but something held him back. After all, the police didn't have to be his first port of call. There were others. Perhaps he could speak to someone from the school, or ask around. There was a pretty music teacher he wouldn't have minded chatting up, except she had recently become engaged to a naval officer and seemed to fantasize about having a flock of children, as many as the von Trapps.

Perhaps he should ask the retired doctor who sometimes showed his face in the pub, and where he would
always tell the same joke. After all, doctors knew a bit
about people. In view of his profession, he would be subject to a duty of confidentiality, but as with time, a duty
of confidentiality was a different entity here on the island.

In the end, Roald decided to pay the family on the Head
a visit. Alone.

He had never been there. It wasn't a place you just
dropped by, unless you had business there, and since Roald
could carry out most repairs himself, he had never needed
a man like Jens Horder.

Horder's carpentry business – or whatever it was he
did – seemed to have ground to a total halt. It was a long
time since the sign down on the main island had been
removed, and the Christmas-tree sales also seemed to have
come to an end. However, the man himself could occasionally be seen with a truckload of junk, and it was said
that he would still turn up at the junkyard or sniff around
a car-boot sale. Sometimes people would actually pay him
to take their junk away.

Roald wondered about the pickup truck, an ancient
Ford F, which should have died a death a long time ago.
Jens Horder had miraculously kept the beast alive. It was
said that the pickup truck used to belong to his father.

Roald had only seen Maria Horder once, several years
ago, when she was waiting at the chemist's. He wouldn't
have known that it was her if it hadn't been for Jens Horder
next to her.

They were an odd couple, the pair of them. They just sat there holding hands, smiling a little shyly without saying a word. Jens Horder's eyes seemed black, inscrutable. He was slim and well shaped – even beautiful, if such a word could be applied to a man – and he was wearing the finest ivory shirt. She, by contrast, had looked rather big next to her husband, but nevertheless she was really pretty. According to regulars at the pub, she had been slim when she arrived on the island. The more Roald furtively studied her from his place in the queue, the prettier she became. Her inscrutability lay in the smile at the corners of her mouth. Then it was Roald's turn to be served.

Recently, however, Jens Horder had started to resemble an unkempt savage, and rumour had it that Maria Horder had grown enormous. At least the postman said so, and he was probably the last person to have seen her on the Head. That was a long time ago now.

Then again, the postman might not be the most reliable of witnesses. For instance, he had more than hinted that Horder received monthly letters from the Mafia containing huge sums of cash. To imagine that Jens Horder was in cahoots with the Mafia was pretty much as far-fetched as implying that the man had killed his own mother. Which was what the postman was also insinuating, though God knows how that idea had got into his head. Perhaps postmen were just prone to fantasizing more than other people because they carried so much information around, so many potential secrets, about which they could speculate but never prove, unless they had X-ray vision.

*

Roald had to come up with an excuse to go to the Head. It wasn't a long trip; all he had to do was cross the Neck. Even so, it felt like quite an expedition.

His acquaintance with Jens Horder was so fleeting that he wasn't even sure that Jens would recognize him. And he couldn't just turn up without a reason. Should he be honest and say that he had seen a boy run towards the Head one night, and wanted to know if Jens and Maria knew anything about it? Perhaps they too had been burgled?

No, he had no wish to refer to the child as a thief and risk getting him into trouble. The boy had enough problems already, whoever he was. Besides, Roald couldn't bear the thought of asking that particular couple about a child.

Perhaps he could invite them to some event at the pub? And then casually ask if they had experienced any breakins, without mentioning anything about the child. No, that was feeble. Jens and Maria Horder were clearly not interested in socializing on the main island. Jens might have been a guest at the pub a long time ago, when Oluf ran it, but only to help Roald's uncle with minor repairs, never to sit in the bar or join in darts nights, or the summer party, or the New Year's Day lunch, or whatever occasion it was that people used as an excuse to drink a little more in slightly smarter clothes. Roald wasn't even sure if Jens Horder drank alcohol, and he had stopped caring about his appearance long ago.

What on earth could he come up with as a pretext for his visit?

The dog. At some point Roald had expressed a desire

to have a dog, and yet he was in two minds about taking on permanent responsibility for an animal. Lars, who usually turned up in the public bar to watch pools football, had told Roald that he was welcome to walk his hunting dog.

Lars suffered from gout and struggled to walk, and his wife never went anywhere but crazy; she had what could most charitably be described as an explosive temper. After she had slapped the postman across the face for turning up with a reminder letter, they had never been known as anything other than Lars and Short Fuse. People knew that she drank a little more than was good for her at home on the farm, but they would obviously never dream of mentioning it. At least not in Lars's presence.

It was a German wirehaired pointer. The kind that looks like an old, distinguished, bearded gentleman, although it was only five years old and its temper was almost as explosive as its mistress's. Its name was Ida.

But she was cute, Ida with the beard. And strong. Lars's instructions were that Roald mustn't let her off the lead until they were well clear of the tarmac road. Roald couldn't wait for that moment to arrive because, after a mere ten minutes of being dragged down the road, his arm was close to dislocating from the shoulder.

As he approached the Neck, he reviewed his mission yet again. He wasn't sure that he knew exactly what he was doing. But taking a dog for a walk up there was OK . . . or was it? He realized that he had no idea if he would be trespassing on private property. All of the Head couldn't belong to Horder, could it? But where was the boundary? Was there even such a thing?

It wasn't just time which had been suspended on the island, Roald had noticed. It was also physical barriers, which seemed to flow rather freely inside the boundaries delineated by the sea. The crops had undulated peacefully between neighbours for generations and boundary posts were mainly located in people's memories.

It would never have worked on the mainland.

There were no crops undulating now, where the November sunshine rose above the landscape, and the golden leaves from a windbreak had long since scattered in the plough furrows on the field he passed.

When the tarmac finally turned into a gravel road, he released the dog. It galloped off over the Neck and on to the Head as if it hadn't stretched out for years, and soon disappeared out of sight.

Perfect. He was looking for his dog, which had done a runner. That was his story. He would ask the Horders if they had seen it, and somehow manage to bring up the child in conversation.

The Neck was quiet. Roald looked down the verges of buckthorn and lyme grass and watched a couple of seagulls fight over a crab. The sea sloshed against the causeway from both sides in small, awkward kisses. To the east there was water, water, water until the sea disappeared in a light mist. To the west the blurred contours of the mainland. He didn't miss it.

\*

And in front of him the Head rose like a broad, dark mass. He felt like Columbus or, better still, Amundsen journeying north. He knew he was being ridiculous, given that the squinting postman came here regularly. It wasn't unexplored territory. But it felt like it.

In the distance, he could hear the dog.

It was screaming.

*An animal is screaming nearby. Is it one of ours? Is it a dog? It sounds like a dog. I don't like it.*

*I don't feel very well, Liv.*

*I wish you could hear what I'm writing. I wish you were here now.*

*What's going on?*

# The Day It Happened

The day it happened I was sitting in the container. It was one of my bad days. That night I had dreamt that I was standing under a waterfall, which changed its mind halfway down. I looked up at all the water suspended right above me, and I knew that any second now it would realize that it couldn't continue hanging there. That only the sea could retreat, not a waterfall. Dad had told me so.

Water falls.

And children drown. Maybe.

When I woke up I tried to carry on with my dream, to turn it into a nice one. I imagined that the waterfall took so long to realize that it was a waterfall that I had time to step back to safety between the rock face and the water, which would soon come crashing down like a heavy blanket. I had read about such things in one of Mum's books: a secret room you could stand in. Behind the curtain.

But as long as I could only imagine it and not dream it, I didn't know if I had truly got myself to a safe place. And I didn't like that feeling.

While I thought about my dream, I mended a hole in my teddy bear. Mum had taught me to sew, just like she had taught me to read. One day I had been given my very own sewing box, which Dad had made and Mum had filled with needles and thimbles and elastic bands and thread. It was with me in the container, right next to my baby sister's coffin.

The teddy bear tended to get holes. And when it did, something white would come out of them. It didn't look like the things that came out of rabbits and deer and foxes and people. This stuff was white and dry and soft and looked like snow when I threw it up into the air before I put it back inside the teddy bear and closed up the hole. I didn't know why the teddy got holes. Perhaps I cuddled it too much, or maybe it was the mice. But at least it wasn't rotting.

Mum was a different matter. And that might have been the real reason I was so sad that day. I had gone to see her with some tinned food, which I had heated on Dad's camping stove. I had also brought her water from the pump. It was easier to get it from the pump than to try to reach the kitchen sink. I would like to have brought her some milk, because she loved fresh milk, but our last cow and the goats didn't produce any now. They needed children to produce milk, Mum had explained. There were no children, and the billy goat had died. It was just lying in the field, stiff as a board, looking way too skinny. I don't know why we didn't take it away. All the animals had started to look skinny. Perhaps they didn't get enough to eat. Dad said he gave them what they needed, but I wasn't so sure . . .

Perhaps it was because their feed was starting to look strange. It smelled odd, too. Some of it was stored in the living room because there was furniture taking up space in the feed store. The gaps between Dad feeding them grew longer and longer, and yet he didn't seem willing to let the animals out to graze any more. I could hear them. I think they were calling out to Dad. Or for grass.

Or maybe they were calling out to me.

But I didn't dare do anything without Dad's permission. And I couldn't pluck up the courage to go to the barn on my own, mostly because I was terrified of what I would find there, I guess.

That morning the noises had been even more mournful than before. I thought I could hear the horse cry.

But it wasn't the animals that had made me the saddest that day. It was Mum.

Mum was also full of holes, but they weren't small, dry openings that I could stitch. They were big, festering sores. When I helped her wash with the flannel and the bowl and she moved about on the mattress, I could see them. They were caused by her lying down so much and being so heavy, she explained to me on her notepad. It was tiny compared to Mum, and the pen practically disappeared inside her hand.

She was so big.

And yet it was as if Mum's body had changed. It distributed itself differently on the bed. It had grown limper – like the teddy bear when too much of the white stuffing had come out of a hole and I hadn't put it back in yet. Perhaps it was because I didn't bring her food as often as I used to. I tried to, but it was difficult. Dad told me not to give her too much.

I no longer knew what Dad was doing. He was there, and at the same time, he wasn't.

The worst thing was that the holes grew worse, and Mum was crying. That morning she had written on her notepad that she had asked Dad to go to the main island. He needed to get something from the chemist to heal her sores. And painkillers. I didn't understand the last part. How did you kill pain? The same way you killed a person? Her handwriting had changed. The sentences had grown shorter, and her handwriting wasn't as neat as it once was.

*Better still, if he could get a doctor*, she added at the end. *We need help now.*

That last line really freaked me out, because Dad had told me about doctors. They were the kind of people you needed to watch out for more than anyone else. They made people sick, he said. And interfered in things they shouldn't. They took people away.

Imagine if they took Mum away. And what about me? What if a doctor came here to visit Mum and saw me? Would he take me away? Make me ill? What if he killed me? I didn't want to die for real.

So I didn't understand what Mum was talking about.

I had also come to the conclusion that I didn't understand Dad either. I understood nothing at all. Carl couldn't help, but it was nice that he was there, so that we could not understand anything together.

I didn't know what I hoped Dad would come back with. I had seen him drive down the gravel road and disappear behind the spruces by the barrier. Before he left, he had taken some money from the money box in the container. The box was jam-packed with banknotes with people and lizards and squirrels and sparrows and fish and butterflies on them, and small brown coins and slightly bigger ones with the face of a lady who could be the butcher's wife in profile.

Dad didn't like money leaving the box. 'We need to look after it, just as we look after you and the things and your baby sister in the coffin.'

I was tempted to add: 'And Mum in the bed and the animals in the barn.' But I didn't.

We also had animals inside the house now. There were rabbits everywhere. I can't imagine where they had come from – we had only had two to begin with. As we always closed and locked the doors, they never came outside unless I took one of them with me to the container. That was the upside to there being so many of them: Dad would never know if one was missing.

Sometimes I wondered what would happen if the rabbits inside the house met the ones outside? Would they be able to talk to each other? I had never been scared of the wild rabbits, but the ones in the house frightened me because there were so many of them. Somehow they seemed wilder than the wild ones.

Then there were the noises they made. When only one of them made a small noise, I didn't mind, but when the whole house grunted, it stopped being nice. And it wasn't just the rabbits making noises; there were other animals: shiny animals darting down the walls and across the floor, where they would make a crunching sound if you accidentally stepped on them. I never did so on purpose. Glossy

blue-green flies buzzed around open cans. Faded butterflies bashed their brown wings against the windowpanes
somewhere behind all the stuff, or where they had been
caught in a web, rotating themselves to death. Small mice
and much bigger mice with very long tails. Something
was always scratching, grunting or squeaking somewhere.
At times it would be Mum.

I had slept in many places around the house. Upstairs in
my own little bedroom, until I could no longer get in
because of all the stuff we kept there. In the furthest room,
until it got too difficult to reach it. With Mum, until there
was no longer room for two people. In the living room, at
the bottom of the stairs, even right inside the door in the
workshop. After all, I could take my duvet anywhere.

But now I nearly always slept in the container with
Carl. It was quiet. At most a few mice would be pottering
about. Small ones. I liked the small ones, but I never for-
gave the one who tried to eat my baby sister.

I slept most of the day. The light felt sharp, so sharp that it
hurt, unless it was mixed with darkness.

I preferred being outside in the moonlight, where the
darkness glowed by itself. Or I would use my torches. I
had them in all sizes and strengths and with many different types of batteries. But whenever I sat in the container,
I lit a pillar candle which I placed inside a small lantern.

I liked watching the flame.

If the container hatch was ajar, or there was a draught
coming from one of the holes Dad had made, the flame
might flatten, get up and twist around itself. The rest of the

time it would just dance around its wick. I tried to imagine the flame hardening like resin, so that millions of years later people would find it, bite it and say: 'Yes, that's an old flame. Once upon a time it was fire.' And a child would be allowed to look inside it and see the ancient wick.

But I couldn't escape the light completely. The daylight. You see, Dad had started sending me into the forest to collect more resin. I drained the trees and I brought back as much as I could – in small buckets which he tipped into the barrels.

'We need more, Liv. Fetch me more. The trees don't mind. Cut holes in more trees. We need more. Much more.'

I didn't know what he was going to do with it all, but I didn't mind because it made him start talking to me again. Even if it was just to ask me for more resin. I was sad that he didn't want to come with me to the forest. I think it would have done him good. I enjoyed being out there, but I missed him. The forest wasn't the same without Dad.

The upside was that he was back in the workshop. Him working on something was much better than him being around without really being present. One day when he had driven to Korsted to fetch something, I went to the workshop to have a look. I was pleased to see that he had tidied up around the workbench, which made it easier for him to move about. There was a pile of planks and I could smell fresh wood. It was so nice that I started to smile. It reminded me of something I liked.

And yet I felt uneasy. Because soon afterwards he came

back with a lot of junk. I also caught a glimpse of a bag of gauze and cans of grapeseed oil.

There was too much of everything.

When I realized what he was making a few days later, it stopped being nice. It was huge. It was many times the size of the tiny coffin he had made for my baby sister.

The day it happened I was sitting in the container, closing up the teddy bear and thinking about the holes and Mum and the waterfall and the money and the rabbits and the doctors and resin and the frozen fire. And Dad's coffin.

That morning I heard a scream.

It wasn't a bird of prey or an owl or a badger or a human being who had just seen a newborn baby die. I had never heard anyone scream like that before, but I was sure that it was an animal. And I was pretty sure that it had to be a dog.

Something inside me told me that it must be caught in a trap. Except that our traps weren't the kind of traps that made you scream; not even in daylight. A fox had once trapped its paw in a rabbit snare at the edge of the forest, but it didn't scream, it was just stuck. I don't think it had been sitting there very long when we found it and freed it. Dad covered its head with his jacket while I cut the string. The fox limped a bit as it ran off, but I think that it was happy. After all, we were kind to animals and we didn't eat foxes.

But this sound. That was an animal in a lot of pain; I could feel it in my tailbone. When I knew that someone was in pain, I would get a long shooting sensation going down to my tailbone, as if my tummy was pulling itself right into my back and down towards the ground. I got the same feeling when I visited Mum and saw her sores.

If Carl had had a real body, I'm sure he would have felt exactly the same – after all, we were twins and inside one another. We had merged together, that was how I saw it. I was a little bit of a boy, and he was a little bit of a girl. Somehow, he was a little bit alive, and I was a little bit dead. Our baby sister was another matter; she was definitely dead. But at least she was here, right next to me, and that made me happy.

It was a terrible scream.

And then I remembered the new traps that Dad had set to keep unwanted visitors at bay – or at least warn us if anyone was coming. I hadn't been allowed to see them all. He had just told me where they were and ordered me never to go near them. And he had looked at me in such a way that I could see that he meant it.

I knew about the three traps along the gravel road, of course. If you followed the path around the barrier when you walked up the gravel road towards the house, you would soon trip over a wire, and it would make some tins close to the house rattle. But tripping over a wire didn't hurt much, did it? Not enough for anyone to scream. And I hadn't heard the tins rattle.

If you somehow managed to evade the tripwire, you would meet another obstacle a little further on. Dad had dug a couple of shallow trenches in the road and covered them with thin pieces of cardboard with gravel and leaves and pine needles on top. If you stepped on the cardboard, your foot would go right into the trench. Now that might hurt a bit, so perhaps you would cry out, but it would also cause some junk to make noise in a nearby tree. That was to warn us. In particular me, so that I would have time to hide.

As you got near the front of the house, there was another trap in the place where most people would choose to walk if they were aiming for the front door. It was another trench, and if you ended up in it, a branch from a nearby tree would swipe your face. But you probably wouldn't get that far before you were discovered.

Dad and I knew exactly where the three traps were so we could avoid ending up in them ourselves. He would park the pickup truck a bit further down the road, opposite the trap at the front of the house. When he got near the second trap with the pickup truck, he would drive half on to the grass so the tyres would go either side of the trench. When I walked there, I'd swerve around a particular spruce so as to stay clear of it. It was the safest way and, no matter how dark it was, I could always find that spruce with my torch. It was much taller than the others, and had a branch sticking out near its top which was easy to see against the sky.

The tripwire down by the barrier was also easy to avoid. All you had to do was not follow the small gravel path. But we were the only ones who knew that. Dad always closed the barrier behind him, even if he was only going out for a quick trip in the pickup truck. He didn't want to run the risk, he said. Anything could go wrong if you weren't careful; if anyone got too close.

Now, like I said, I didn't know anything about the

other traps, the new ones. All I knew was never to take the path left around the juniper bush in order to reach the house, or walk between the tall birches before the thicket, or down the path through the scrub south of the house. If you chose to ignore the gravel road, which was the most obvious route, then they were the most likely ones.

There were also certain places around the farmyard where I wasn't allowed to go, and Dad had given me routes to follow in between the piles. Unless I followed them, I would cause terrible damage, he said. I didn't know how, but I didn't want to cause terrible damage, so I always did exactly as he said – except for taking a rabbit to the container. And also because he had looked at me with those eyes as he said it. I could tell from them that it was very important.

Now the sound changed from a scream to a howl, which grew inside my head. I stared out through the peepholes in the container and held my breath. My heart was pounding so hard that I could hear that too.

And then I spotted it. Down by the juniper bush. Something was moving. It looked like a dog, a big dog, but I only saw it in flashes when it threw itself to one side.

We were supposed to be kind to animals. I was kind to animals. And the dog couldn't possibly have come to take me away. But it might bite me. I was a bit scared of dogs because they had teeth, and because I believed that Dad was a bit scared of them too. He had certainly always avoided visiting any houses with dogs that might make a noise.

OK, so we had been able to visit the insurance salesman, because his dog, which was very long as well as having long ears, never made a sound if we gave it some wine gums. I wasn't sure that it could get up from its spot by the door to the pantry, even if it wanted to. But it would wag its tail non-stop, and the trick was to put a long, thick sock around it straightaway so it wouldn't make a noise when it bashed it against the floor. Once we forgot to take the sock off its tail before we left and that caused such a fuss that Dad heard about it when he was queuing in the post office a few days later: the insurance salesman had been showing the sock at the pub. And it turned out to be a sock which the chemist's wife had knitted for her husband – one of a pair, I mean. Now the chemist was accusing the insurance salesman of having nicked his priceless socks, and the insurance sales-man accused the chemist of having treated his Basset hound badly. We still have the other sock somewhere. We must take good care of it.

Then it struck me that the howling dog might be heard as far as the main island. Perhaps Dad could hear it, wherever he was. Perhaps lots of doctors would come running and make us ill or take me away if they heard it.

I had to stop the howling.

My bow lay near me in the container. I put the teddy bear away and reached for it. And my quiver. Everything was ready for action, only my bow hadn't seen much use recently, because we didn't eat that kind of food any more. Tins were easier, Dad said. But I still practised from time to time.

As I ran down towards the juniper bush, I discovered that I had been crying, but also that I had stopped. My eyes stung a little. Or perhaps it was the daylight.

My heart was still pounding, but the rest of my body was doing what I told it to. I jumped silently over grassy knolls and zigzagged between the small trees, which were shooting up everywhere, like a forest for very small people. My baby sister would probably think the trees were tall. I could see across them as I ran. The quiver slapped my back softly with every jump; I had made it myself with the pelts from four wild rabbits. And I had moulded the tips and turned the arrows, while Dad told me everything about what wood could do and smiled at everything his daughter could do.

The dog was lying on its side, and the howling had become long and high-pitched, as if it were about to run out. But it was there. Like an ice pick in my ear.

Horrified, I stared at its hind leg, which lay twisted on the grass. The lower part was trapped in a metal monster, which seemed to be fixed with a chain somewhere in the ground under the grass and the twigs. Although the grass was taller here, there was a natural passage between the juniper bush and some trees. This was a place I wasn't allowed to go. One of them. The metal monster looked like a giant set of teeth which had snapped around the dog's hind leg. The dog had made some attempts to free its leg, but every time the big teeth seemed to sink deeper into its flesh. Its blood was very red in the daylight. There was way too much light. And way too much blood. I'd never seen anything as red as that blood.

I tried. I really tried my best to pull the metal teeth apart, but I couldn't. I also tried twisting them apart with a branch, but it snapped. The metal was super-strong.

I started crying again. And I looked at the dog lying on its side, watching me. I looked at its teeth, which were disappearing in white foam. Its tongue hung limply down on the grass. This dog wasn't going to bite me, no matter how scared it was. It was desperate for help.

Its chest was heaving and sinking in front of me. It was almost as if the howling was coming from in there. I took a step back, got ready and aimed. It was my best arrow.

I'm sure I shot it straight through the heart. I looked into its eyes and, for a brief moment, the dog and I were as one.

Then it was dead.

I hadn't decided what I was going to do next. Nor did I have time because, as soon as the howling stopped, I heard shouting.

'Ida!' someone called out in the distance. A man. 'Iiiida!'

I ran faster than I've ever done. Although I wanted to run straight back to the container more than anything, I didn't dare because the man might spot me crossing the open area, and I didn't know how much time I had. So instead I decided to run the shorter distance to the edge of the forest. I could hide between the tall trees and, if he decided to follow me, I could lose him in the forest. Whoever he was, he wouldn't know the forest as well as I did.

I found the spot where I would be completely hidden by pine branches but still have a good view down towards the juniper bush. I could see him now. He wore a big, green coat – and he had something around his neck. I think it was a lead. It was probably his dog.

I was sure that I had seen him before, but I couldn't remember where. I had never seen the dog. I hoped that he had been good to his dog, but people down on the main island probably weren't as kind to animals as we were. Seeing as they weren't particularly kind to people.

I tried not to think that it was my dad who had made that metal trap and set it. But I couldn't get it out of my mind.

What if the man was a doctor? But surely Dad wouldn't have . . . ? And who was Ida? Was that the dog? I hadn't even noticed if it was female. But it had a beard, a grey beard. White almost. I hoped that it was an old dog.

The man was kneeling by it now. He was saying something to it, I could see. He stroked it. And wiped its mouth. And tried to prise the metal teeth apart with his hands. And he gently pulled out the arrow. And he pressed his face to the dog's chest. And he sat up again and looked at it. And he spotted the long end of the branch I had used and tried separating the metal teeth from one another with the branch. Until it snapped. Again. And he shook his head.

I think he was crying.

I saw him get up. He dried his eyes on his sleeve and stared at the dog for ages. Then he bent down, picked up my arrow and spent a long time staring at it. It looked as if he was examining it, and I hoped that he would think that it was a really fine arrow. I had worked very hard on it.

Then he turned and looked up towards our house. From where he was standing, he could see the container and, behind it, the wooden building with the workshop and the white room. There was a single small window into the white room, but I knew it was impossible to see anything through it. To the left of the workshop the man would probably see the roof of the house. There was a cluster of spruces and birches that gave some privacy. The gravel road ran alongside them and disappeared into the corner between the house and the workshop before the yard began. The yard where, it has to be said, there was very little free space these days.

I wondered why he hadn't just walked up the gravel road. He should have reached the barrier and either turned around there when he saw our sign or followed the path around the barrier in order to walk on up to the house. Then he would have come into contact with the tripwire and there would have been a noise . . . And that was when it dawned on me that he had followed the sound, the howling. The dog must have run in an arc away from the barrier and the gravel road, and up towards the Christmas trees and the north forest. It might have been chasing a wild rabbit; I knew there was a rabbit warren near the place where I was hiding.

I also wondered what would have happened if it hadn't been the dog but the man who had stepped on the metal trap and been doing the screaming. And if I would have shot him in the heart until he stopped.

And if Dad had made any more of those traps.

I hoped the man would go back. I hoped with all my heart that he would leave and take the dog with him, although I couldn't see how, because it was trapped and the trap was fixed to the ground. And I hoped that he would leave my arrow behind.

He left the dog and took my arrow and walked up towards the container.

I held back for a while. Then I followed him, hidden by the trees.

*Liv, the noise has stopped. It's so very quiet.*

*It is making my mind loud.*

*I hurt all over. It's the sores, they are on fire. And my hands, mostly the right one.*

*Difficult to write now.*

*Perhaps I've started to believe in God. I would like to believe in something. In someone. I believe in you.*

*Is that a voice?*

# One Big Mess

Roald had once seen a fox trap. It was a fiendish contraption, but this one . . . it was far worse. Someone had taken a fox trap and refined it in an effort to turn it into the worst imaginable instrument of torture. The metal teeth had practically severed the dog's lower leg. Just imagine the damage such a trap could have done to a human being. It was big enough to snap a grown man's leg, not to mention a child's. What if the boy he had seen run north in the darkness had stepped in it?

Roald shuddered at the thought and tried to swallow. The lump he had felt in his throat when he heard Ida howl was choking him now. The poor, poor animal.

And poor Short Fuse's Lars. What was he going to tell him?

He couldn't even take Ida back until he had found something with which to cut the chain; it seemed to be fastened around an underground root. Who the hell would deliberately do something so cruel? It might be kinder to Short Fuse's Lars to cut off the dog's leg, so that he would never have to see the trap and the injuries it had caused.

But there was more than that. It wasn't just the trap.

There was also the arrow.

How come the dog had an arrow through its heart? An

arrow which had evidently been made lovingly by hand, right down to the smallest detail.

He had to find Horder to get an explanation. Could Jens Horder have set the trap himself? He undoubtedly had the skill to make it, but did he also have the heart not only to make it but also to use it? Anyone who set a device like that must have a heart of stone.

Was it malice? Was Jens Horder an evil man? Judging by what people had told him about Jens, quite the opposite. Kind and helpful, gentleness personified. And behind the gentleness, clearly devastated by the loss of his twins. He might be an introverted and monosyllabic man, but that wasn't a sign of malice, was it? Surely he must be a frightened man, to retreat and put in place emotional and physical barriers to prevent people from getting too close.

But traps? Such vile, cruel traps?

Roald looked up towards the Horder home. It consisted of several buildings and a big, closed skip stood in front of one of them. The postman had mentioned the skip repeatedly and gone on about how Jens Horder was hiding Mafia money inside it. Or worse. Of everyone who drank at the pub, the postman was the only one who insisted on drinking nothing but Red Tuborg; then again, he was a few stamps short of full postage. Still, in his own way, he was the most entertaining too. Roald, for his part, wouldn't want to be without him. The others had merely proffered dull theories about how perhaps the Horders had finally decided to get rid of some of their stuff up on the Head, and not a moment too soon.

Except for the postman, no one really spoke about Jens and Maria Horder these days. Then there was the whole subject of the drowned daughter; that made it difficult for most people to talk about the couple. It wasn't enough to be separated from the tragedy by a thin strip of land. Tragedies take time.

Roald wondered whether to make his way down to the gravel road and then follow it up towards the house, but in the end opted to take a direct route. The risk of stumbling across more traps was surely the same in either case, so he kept an eye out for where he put his feet between the small trees, the grassy knolls and the twigs.

He paused only when a rabbit jumped past him on its way to the forest. More than anything, he wanted to run back towards the Neck, but he knew he had no choice but to carry on.

The memory of the boy in his kitchen still haunted him.

Once he got closer to the skip, he could see how old and battered it was. It had probably been cheap, and it was unlikely to be rented, given how long it had sat there, according to the postman. It had slanted walls and hatches along the top.

Roald walked around it. There was a gap of a couple of metres at most between the skip and the wooden building behind it. There was little actual clear space because there was junk everywhere. The nearest hatch was unlocked, and he opened it to look inside. The skip was filled practically to the brim with what looked, undeniably, like rubbish.

The postman was unlikely to be right in his bizarre assumptions.

It would have made sense to walk the short stretch along the skip to the end of the house, but the small window at the far end of the wooden building that overlooked the forest piqued Roald's curiosity. He decided to explore what was behind it.

He had to step blindly in between wooden posts and hubcaps and sheets of tarpaulin and collapsed log piles before he could reach it. All the time, he prayed that a set of metal teeth wouldn't suddenly snap shut around his foot.

But he could have saved himself the trouble. Behind the windowpane, it was as if someone had constructed a wall of densely packed books and compressed rubbish, and even if all the lights in the world had been lit up beyond it, they still wouldn't have been able to penetrate it. Down on the small windowsill, squashed between the glass and a tinfoil tray, was a dusty hairbrush matted with blond hair. Next to it was something that had once been a plant.

Roald decided to walk around the end of the house which was nearest to him, and as he glanced towards the spruces, he thought he spied movement. He stopped and narrowed his eyes, but he couldn't make out what it was. He was still holding the arrow in his hand and suddenly felt unpleasantly exposed. After all, someone had fired that arrow, not that long ago.

Whatever he might have seen behind the wooden building was nothing compared to the sight he encountered in the farmyard. Shocked, he stared at the forest of rubbish shooting up everywhere. A red silage harvester soared above it all. It reminded him of a dinosaur looking across a landscape of prehistoric junk.

And it wasn't the only animal. Roald shuddered when he spotted a rat making a dash for a steel tube. Faint sounds could be heard everywhere whenever the breeze caused something to lift or bump into something else. A piece of transparent plastic flapped under a wooden pallet, the cardboard tube from a roll of toilet paper unfurled itself in front of a tarnished copper pot. The wooden building to his right was actually rather beautiful, but blighted by its surroundings. There was a door and a window near him, and further down another couple of windows and a door. At the end of the farmyard, the main house rose in the morning sun. Painted white, but peeling so badly you could be forgiven for having doubts that it had ever been painted. The curtains on the ground floor were closed, but from the first floor two windows glared at Roald like a blind animal with pitch-black eyes covered by a milky membrane.

If he was to reach the front door, he would have to zigzag between the piles because there didn't seem to be a direct route. Some noises made him turn his attention to the barn across the farmyard. It was a stone building in just as poor condition as the house. Despite a thick layer of moss, the corrugated-iron roof looked far from waterproof. Could they really be keeping animals in there?

Roald decided to walk around the piles and up to the half-door at the end of the barn. The top half was ajar, and in the darkness he saw a horse. Dappled grey. Its far too skinny neck and head hung over the edge of its stall, as if held in place, barely, by an invisible rope. A faint whinnying was coming from its nostrils. He could hear more animals inside the barn. Something shifted, something breathed, something squeaked. He had no wish to investigate. The acrid stench not only suggested that mucking out was long overdue but also that something inside there was dead.

From behind the barn he heard another pitiful sound, and he walked around to see what it was. In the chicken coop a solitary cockerel with miserable plumage was trying to communicate. Its eyes seemed dead, probably because it was looking at his dead fellows on the ground: five ruffled chickens whose eyes were just as empty. He could see that a fox had tried to tunnel its way under, but the chicken coop seemed to have been secured against that kind of attack. Perhaps it would have been more merciful if the chickens had ended their days with a sudden death.

There was a field beyond the chicken coop, but the only things moving out there were a couple of crows and three black plastic bin liners rolling languidly across the autumn grass whenever the wind caught them. Further away lay something which might be a dead, horned animal. Or maybe just the remains of one; whatever it was, it didn't move.

Roald walked along the field, past the pump and the upended wheelbarrow, straddled some big stones and old tubs, and approached the back of the house. There was a washing line with a fluttering newspaper and a couple of yellowing, torn sheets on it. An impressive rosebush next to it stretched its branches up into the wind like tentacles, waiting for the next crumbling bedsheet. It was a little windy here, where the forest didn't provide quite so much shelter.

At the end of the house was a door with a window-pane, only partly covered by a piece of fabric. It was dark inside, but he got the impression that it led to some kind of pantry.

He hesitated for a moment. Would he be better off walking around and knocking on the front door? Should he do that? Then again, the place seemed so deserted it surely didn't matter what he did. With his hands up around his eyes, he pressed his nose to the windowpane. When his eyes had adjusted to the darkness, he spotted his missing freezer gloves from the pub's stock room. They were lying on top of some bubble wrap, which he also recognized, and nearby was that roll of oilcloth he had bought at the ironmonger's in Sønderby. It gave him a strange feeling that he was entitled to enter.

He grabbed the door handle. The door was locked and he knocked a few times, without expecting an answer. Then he took a step back and looked about him. It was here, the key. Somewhere. There was always a key. On a nail behind something. Under a flower pot. A stone. Or placed on top of a beam.

It turned out to be under the flower pot.

The door didn't open without a struggle. The hinges needed oiling and squealed hideously. Roald let out a star-tled gasp when some kind of furry animal passed him in the doorway, brushing his leg. He followed it with his eyes as it bounced out into the grass and breathed a sigh of relief when he realized that it wasn't a giant rat but just a rabbit.

A tame rabbit? Should he try to catch it, in case it turned out to be someone's pet? He didn't have time to make up his mind before the rabbit vanished among the grass and the junk and he lost sight of it. That decided it.

The air inside was more oppressive than any air in any house he had ever set foot in.

And yet it was nothing compared to the smell. The stench. It materialized in his nose as an intolerable mixture of dust, mould, decay and solvents and . . . he feared . . . urine, excrement. He opened the door fully so that he could stand it. Now that a little daylight was entering the room, he was better able to see what it concealed. There was every imaginable kind of tinned food stacked randomly or in boxes. Some were still held together by shrink-wrapped plastic. And there were packets of cereal, crispbread, bags of bread, crackers. He didn't need to check the best-before date to know that they were way past it. Pretty much all the bread he could see through the packaging was green from mould. He picked up his stockroom gloves, but dropped them immediately as mouse droppings rolled from them, scattering on to the bubble wrap like dry rain.

The light switch clicked impotently when he flicked it, and the naked lightbulb over the door remained unlit. When he discovered the chest freezer along one wall he knew where the worst of the smell was coming from.

There was no light glowing in the small indicator lamp on the side of the freezer, but he had no doubts that it contained food, because there was a terrible stench of rotting meat.

Roald breathed a sigh of relief when he realized that he wouldn't be able to check whether he was right because the chest freezer was buried under things, including an enormous old television that must weigh a ton. The dust on the television was thick, and he didn't want to think about how long the freezer had been turned off.

Again, he wondered whether he should leave. He ought to hurry back to Korsted and get hold of the police officer and the vet. The vet could see not only to the animals in the barn but also to dead Ida. Roald no longer had the strength to deal with the dog in the trap himself. Someone else would have to take over. He discovered that he was no longer holding the arrow. He must have put it down outside, by the flower pot.

It beggared belief. No one could possibly live like this, and yet *someone* must come here. The boy, for instance, since his recent swag was locked inside this room.

But who had fired the arrow?

And where were Jens Horder and his wife? There was no one here to tend to the animals, and the house seemed completely dark and closed up, as if it had been abandoned long ago. But they couldn't have moved, or the postman would know.

And that was when Roald remembered a call he had once had at the pub. It had been during the herring course of their New Year's Day's lunch, so he hadn't paid much attention and he might not have been entirely sober. But someone had asked about Jens Horder, and possibly also about his mother. Roald could remember nothing more than that.

A second door led into the house, probably to a kitchen. He wasn't sure if he had the courage to open it. No, he decided that it was time to call in the professionals. There were limits to what he, as one man, should stick his nose into, although he had come no closer to understanding the mystery of the boy in the last half-hour.

But he might as well knock on the front door on his way back. He was pretty sure there would be no answer, so it was mostly so he could tell himself he had at least tried that too. Tried. Half-heartedly.

He turned to leave, and it wasn't until then that he heard them. The sounds. He had been so busy breathing and coping with the stench while trying to think clearly at same time that his hearing must have gone into hibernation. But now he heard them. All around him something was creeping and scratching and munching. A particularly loud packet of cornflakes was moving slightly on the shelf in front of him.

Roald stared at it. Now he could also hear faint squeaking. Rats? The thought that the house might be riddled with rats made him jumpy. Mice, he could handle, or a mouse. But rats, hell no.

He took another step towards the external door but was stopped by a sudden, troubling thought. What if someone was in there? Roald had once had a friend who had never forgiven himself for ignoring the silence from the flat next door to his and the junk mail piling up outside. He had also blocked out the stench to begin with. After all, people were entitled to their privacy, that had been his friend's thinking. They found the old man three weeks too late. On the living-room floor. He seemed to have died as he crawled towards the telephone.

Was Jens Horder lying in there dead? Or his wife? Was there even anybody in there? And what was the boy's part in all of this? Who was he? Where did he fit in?

Roald rubbed his chin. He decided to steel himself. Or at least call out from where he was standing.

So he did.

A standard 'Hello?'

And he noticed that all the noises stopped for a moment, only to return, somewhat tentatively.

And he called out again. 'Hello, is anyone there? Hellooooo?'

He sounded more at ease than he felt.

By his third 'Hello', the noises had grown used to him. A dark shadow slipped past a tin on a shelf. A small, dark shadow, thank God. As long as they were just mice, it was OK. A small mouse . . . preferably a shrew.

Which wasn't a mouse at all, according to the plumber.

'Helloooo . . . ?'

But some kind of mole.

There was no response except from the animals. So he might as well leave, mightn't he? Or should he just check inside the kitchen?

*

The two rabbits that slipped out this time did nothing to calm his nerves. He felt as if they had been lying in wait behind the kitchen door. They dashed past him, out through the pantry, into the light and across the field. Roald closed the door behind him without quite knowing why. Was he scared of letting too much out of a home he had no right to enter? Too many pets.

It had said *No trespassing* on the sign down by the barrier. But, for pity's sake, he had just lost a dog in a horrible way near this property, and his floral oilcloth was in the pantry. That definitely gave him cause to enter. He was entitled to know what was going on.

Or did it say *No entry*? Suddenly, he had doubts.

There wasn't much light in the kitchen because the faded brown curtains in front of the window overlooking the farmyard were closed. Even so, a little of the daylight pierced the fabric and cast a strange golden glow into the room. The smell was just as foul as in the pantry, and Roald had to pinch his nose. There was also a fridge, containing God knows what. He had no desire to investigate it further, especially after he had tried the light switch just inside the door and discovered that there was no working light in the kitchen either.

Again, it was almost impossible for him to move about because of boxes, and stuff, and all kinds of rubbish. It was impossible to reach the door at the far end of the kitchen, which was blocked by a big crate of engine parts. Roald guessed the door led to the hallway. It fitted with the location of the front door.

With the help of an otherwise useless umbrella, he

managed to reach the curtain across the junk, pull it slightly to one side and let in more light. He regretted his decision immediately when he saw what it revealed: the dusty cobwebs that covered everything like a sticky, grey membrane, the dead, dying and still-living spiders and cockroaches, and all sorts of creepy-crawlies populating the room from floor to ceiling.

An open box of Liquorice Allsorts lit up the place with its fresh colours and simple shapes. It looked as if it had been left there recently. His favourites had always been the pink coconut wheels, but surely they tasted exactly the same as the yellow ones? On the wall was a faded poster of different species of fish staring at him with their dead eyes. Roald looked down before taking his next step. More sweets. A half-empty bag of wine gums had landed in a flower pot and someone seemed to have emptied a bag of salt-liquorice balls across the floor.

Salt liquorice? How unusual.

And when he bent down to take a closer look, he discovered that the droppings in the dust weren't Haribo, but from the rabbits. Their excrement was everywhere. Could three rabbits really produce that much poo?

Four.

Because, as he straightened up and accidentally kicked a hubcap, yet another rabbit jumped out from its hiding place. It disappeared through a half-open door to his right, leading to the living room, perhaps.

The noises increased in number. And volume.

He decided to take a quick look inside the living room and then get the hell out of here. It was all too much, but one thought troubled him more than anything: he wasn't sure that he could cope if he discovered a dead body inside the house. Better send the police out here. And then there was the air. It was suffocating. It was so dense with dust he felt the urge to cough the whole time. And somewhere in the back of his mind was the knowledge that the dog had been killed by an arrow which someone had fired not that long ago. Someone unlikely to be dead.

And yet his conscience compelled him to look inside. Just a quick peek before he left. He cautiously opened the door a little more. Yes, it was a living room. Or it had been once.

A wall of things had risen in front of the south-facing windows at the far end of the room. Rays of sunlight were trying to get through the cracks in the wall and into the room, but on their way through the dust they faded to weak shadows unable to produce anything other than a pale imitation of light.

Roald felt like he had entered an underground mine shaft. He was standing in a narrow passage that wound its way through the objects, which had merged together into what at first glance looked like one dark mass. Now he tried to make out the contours that slowly emerged from the twilight. He saw umbrellas, again. A stuffed owl. At least, he hoped it was stuffed. In several places the junk almost reached the ceiling. He took a step forwards and saw a piano to one side. A bust, an upended sofa, a tailor's dummy, a dining table, barrels, clothes, plastic bags, cardboard packaging. It went on. A couple of other paths appeared.

Stunned, he stared at an object hanging from the ceiling. It looked like a tree stripped of its leaves – a hanging spruce? It was a Christmas tree; he could see the star now. And the paper-heart decorations. Some were close to falling off the bare branches; others had already done so. One of them released its grip as he approached. The paper hearts looked strangely dull but, on the other hand, the darkness probably didn't leave much room for colour. The crunchy sound of spruce needles under the soles of his shoes roused his sense of hearing. The sounds. There was scratching and scurrying all around him.

He had to get out, and it couldn't happen soon enough. And given that he had already moved some way through the living room, probably in the direction of the hall, he would continue that way. It couldn't be worse than having to walk back past the fridge and the freezer. Roald cursed himself for having ventured so far inside the house; for even entering the house in the first place.

When his path was blocked by a big canvas sack and he tried to push it aside three startled rabbits hopped away and disappeared in the darkness. As he picked up the sack to move it he could feel its contents trickle out over one of his shoes from a hole in the bottom. He set it down, retracted his foot and looked at it. Animal feed had settled like a small mountain range across the path, and the now slack canvas sack collapsed to one side.

He straddled the mountains and continued along the narrow path. He felt the need to support himself against the bulging walls on either side, not least because he feared that something might come crashing down on top of him, but at the same time he didn't want to touch anything. The thought of feeling a rat against the palm of his hand made him shudder. He held up his hands to each side, not touching anything, but ready to grab out for support.

And then they came.

Maybe he had knocked the sack into something when he moved it a moment ago, but whatever it was had triggered a collapse behind him. He jumped at the sound of things cascading and falling and sliding and crashing into one another. When he turned, he saw the whole of one side of the room cave in. The owl fell. A big old radio tumbled over the edge, pulling with it something from the other side as it did so. Some cardboard slipped down, and a sack . . . and a little light crept in. But only a ray.

An image of avalanches popped into his head. Mudslides. Would everything come tumbling from behind and bury him alive? Death by suffocation?

And then *they* came. The rabbits. From every hole and corner and crack. Roald clutched his head and screamed as he tried to outrun the panicking pets.

The path was widening slightly now. He had a choice between running up the stairs, where a narrow passage had been created down the middle, or following the route to his left, through the hall, across to the front door . . .

He skidded to a halt.

The rabbits had gathered in small clusters, most of them in the corner behind the stairs under a go-kart. The noise had stopped.

He realized that it hadn't been an avalanche, just a minor collapse. All the fallen items had settled themselves again. Behind them, in a thick beam of liberated sunlight, the dead tree hung like a silent witness.

Roald looked about him. There was slightly more light at this end of the living room, thanks to a small window up on the landing. It must be the east-facing end of the house.

Then a short section of the wall between the hall and the kitchen caught his attention. Down by the skirting board there was a fairly large hole with a jagged edge. The furry inhabitants of this house must have gnawed their way through the wall. A cable with protruding copper wire stuck out, it looked like a confused caterpillar, and on the floor in front of the hole bits of insulation lay scattered between excrement and scraps of wallpaper. Something similar had happened to the wall by the stairs, and Roald dreaded to think what other surprises might be revealed if the walls were stripped. The wiring consti-tuted a fire hazard. And how much more gnawing and nibbling could the house cope with before the whole place caved in?

His musings were brutally interrupted by the sight of a rat darting across the floor.

'*Out*,' he ordered it, pointing to the corner as if he expected the rat to obey his command. The creature dis-appeared in another direction, but he could still see the end of its tail sticking out behind a wellington boot.

And that was when he heard it.

A knocking was coming from the first floor. It wasn't an animal making a noise or a bird pecking or the wind

causing something to slam. It was a human being knocking. It was a human being who wanted to be heard.

The trip up the stairs was a nightmare. One of those where
you try to run but can only move forwards in slow motion.
Perhaps the dust was hampering him. The heavy air. The
stench. Roald's lungs were screaming for fresh air, but he
had to go upstairs. He didn't want to suffocate in this
place, but neither, as a decent human being, could he walk
away.

The boy might be up there and in need of his help.

When he reached the first-floor corridor, he saw a light
flicker from the nearest room. From where the sound was
coming. A couple of rabbits pressed themselves against
some long iron girders as he passed them to reach the
door.

Roald had never seen a human being that big before. She
was lying on a bed. That is to say, Roald presumed that
she was lying on a bed. He could barely see the bed for
notepads, books, paper plates, foil trays, knitting, wax
candles, matches, paper cups, filthy towels, holey blankets,
food scraps, mouse droppings – please let them be mouse
droppings, he prayed. And body, body, body.

The air was intolerable, but the stench coming from
her was unbearable. An unmistakable smell of urine and
excrement. And rot. Roald fought to quell his nausea.

She was holding an umbrella in her right hand. She was
slamming its handle against the headboard, and he realized that was how she had made the knocking sound.

When she saw him standing in the doorway she let go of the umbrella and allowed her enormous arm to fall on to some knitting with what looked like extreme fatigue.

On a bedside table, on top of piles of books and papers, a wax candle sputtered in a holder. Roald's joy at finding a source of light was quickly replaced by horror at the state of the room it was illuminating.

Mostly, however, at the woman lying in front of him.

She was in a terrible state.

'Maria Horder?' he asked, in a voice he no longer recognized as his own. Perhaps it was the dust.

She nodded slowly.

'I . . . you, I . . . what are . . . ?' Roald found himself unable to think straight. 'I'm Roald Jensen from the pub in Korsted,' he managed to say, eventually.

The woman's features seemed tiny in the massive face, but he had no doubt that she was attempting a friendly smile. Nor was he in any doubt that she was crying, even though he could only just make out her eyes in the black holes. Her skin looked grey in the guttering candlelight and a grotesque shadow from her nose settled across one cheek like a small, trembling animal.

'You need help,' he stated.

She nodded again.

'I'll go and get someone. But where's your husband . . . Where is Jens Horder?' His brain was starting to work again.

She reached for a notepad with her left hand, pushed aside the novel lying on her stomach and started writing something. He saw *Madame Bovary* slide into a foil tray.

Roald stepped forward to read her note; that is to say, he stepped across a lot of things to get close enough.

COMING SOON, NEED MEDICINE, DOCTOR, she had written. It was clearly a great effort for her to write. That it used not to be, he could tell from the many loose sheets lying scattered everywhere. Some were covered in a beautiful curved handwriting, others were not quite so elegant. Her handwriting now was bordering on a child's scribbles.

'Yes, I'll be quick . . .'

SAVE LIV, she wrote, and stared at him with pleading eyes.

He nodded, wondering if she had trouble spelling. Did she want him to save her *life*?

'I promise, I'll . . . I'll be back as soon as I can. Be careful not to knock over the candle . . .'

She gestured to indicate it was very important that she gave him more information before he left. Her exhaustion was plain to see. It struck him that she might not have had anything to drink for a long time.

WATCH OUT FOR TRAPS.

He nodded. Oh, yes.

'Would you like me to fetch you some water before I go?' he asked anxiously. He caught a glimpse of a hand-drawn sketch of two children on the wall behind her.

She shook her head and wrote again. She added a FIRST . . . after SAVE LIV. A whining sound came from her lungs.

NEED HELP ALL 3.

Roald couldn't take the stench any more. He had to get

out before he threw up. He had a horrible realization of what was in the bucket standing beside the bed. There were sheets of toilet paper and rolled-up towels next to it.

He didn't dare open his mouth to speak, but he nodded, then turned towards the door. It was only compassion that stopped him from vomiting before he was back in the living room, and then he did it as quietly as possible – into a cardboard box whose contents were unknown.

All three? Did she mean that the boy was theirs? And whose life should he save first?

Roald reached the front door and pulled it open so hard that it slammed into the wall. He had never needed fresh air as badly as he did now. He stepped outside and drew the light into his soul and the November sky deep into his lungs.

He spotted it purely by chance, the top of what looked like a quiver; a small collection of neat feathers moving for a brief second behind a bathtub over by the barn. Roald narrowed his eyes.

'Oi, you!' he yelled. 'You over by the bathtub, I saw you.' The next moment a child ran as if the devil were at its heels from the bathtub and along the barn in a semicircle towards the forest and the end of the wooden building from where Roald himself had come. The quiver bounced up and down the back of the brown-and-orange sweater.

Roald recognized the boy from the pub kitchen.

From the top step he could see that there was a more direct route across the farmyard. If he ran past the silage harvester, he might be able to catch up with the child.

*SOMEONE WAS HERE*
*YOU WILL GET HELP, LIV*

*I LOVE YOU BOTH*
*SO MUCH*

# Nightmares

They had started when he burned his mother's body behind the barn. Jens Horder's nightmares.

First he dreamt that Else came back with a schoolteacher, a police officer and a doctor and took Liv away. He was busy mucking out the barn and didn't notice anything until it was too late. He had time to see them get into a big car parked in the farmyard and drive off so fast that dust rose from the gravel road like thick fog. Jens ran into the dust, and when he came out of it he had reached the start of the Neck – but the land itself was gone. The sea had overwhelmed the Neck, and he could do nothing but watch as the car disappeared into the sunshine on the main island.

Jens woke up the moment he ran out into the sea and felt the water fill his lungs.

And the nightmares grew more complex.

They came back: his mother, the doctors, the teachers, the police. Over time, they morphed into anonymous people, random faces he had seen somewhere. What they had in common was that they all wanted to rob him of everything that mattered to him.

In one dream he was out by the Christmas trees and, when he came back, they had taken everything: Liv, Maria, the animals, the buildings, his things. It was all gone. He saw some people running away, and he chased after them, but nothing could stop them. He kept tripping over grassy knolls, roots and trees, which shot up everywhere in front of him, while the others met with no obstacles. They never stumbled. They increased their lead and always made it to the main island. When he finally reached the Neck, it was cut off by the sea every time. He was all alone on a deserted island.

In one of the really bad dreams they turned up in white coats, wanting to take Maria. They were there, in her room, when Jens returned from a night-time visit to Korsted; they were standing around her with saws and scalpels, pointing big lights at her. They were going to take her with them, they said, so that they could help her. But she was far too big and heavy to get out of the door, so they were forced to cut her up into smaller pieces. Once they had got her out of the house and far away from Jens, they would help her, they kept assuring him.

Jens always tried to wake up. But he couldn't. And he couldn't stop them. They had already cut off her head and placed it on the bedside table. Maria looked at him with her beautiful eyes and mouthed that she loved him. Despite the smile at the corner of her mouth, she was crying, and sometimes her limbs on the bed would twitch, as if protesting at being severed. There was no blood. She was like china. Her hand kept clutching the pen when it was leaned up against the doorframe, along with the rest of her arm.

Then they cut her torso into smaller sections, and he pleaded with them not to touch her heart. 'We'll take good care of her,' they kept on saying. 'We can take better care of her than you can, Jens Horder.'

He stared at them as they transported her out of the room, one piece at a time. He was allowed to carry her head. 'I love you,' he whispered into her ear. Her head was heavy, horribly heavy. But the worst part was that Maria's body began to disintegrate as they moved it downstairs. Jens was walking behind the doctor who was holding her right leg, and he could see how it was starting to crumble. The same was happening to the other parts of her body. Her heart fell out of a piece of torso and rolled down the stairs until it hit the landing, like a puffball mushroom deflating. Finally, her head disintegrated as well. Jens couldn't hold on to her. He looked into her eyes before they disappeared between his fingers, and she was gone. Turned to dust.

'Right, we'll take your daughter instead,' they said. 'By the way, does she have any brothers or sisters?'

Yet again the intruders disappeared towards the Neck with their catch, and Jens couldn't stop them. He kept stumbling, getting caught in something. It was as if the forces of nature had ganged up against him. They blocked his path and terrified him. The forest, the sea, the animals . . . they were no longer his friends.

The intruders ran on unabashed.

All he wanted to do was to stop them.

Jens always woke up bathed in sweat and tears. His waking hours, however, were also plagued by nightmares – thoughts of what had been and what might happen next. In the end, he could no longer tell the difference.

# The Postman

The postman was in a particularly good mood that morning. And he had to admit to having a butterfly or two in his tummy, although it wasn't the season for that kind of thing.

He had business at the Head.

For the first time ever, the letter from M had been sent by registered post. The postman wondered sorely at this sudden upgrade in the postage but was nevertheless delighted at being given an outlet for his curiosity. Surely he could now allow himself to enquire about the sender – who might not be a Mafioso after all, however much he wanted to hang on to the thought.

He would especially like to know if 'M' was the same as 'M – Inventions for Life', which was listed as the sender on the big parcel he was also delivering to Jens Horder that day. The business had a mainland address, a place on the east coast. The postmarks on the two items were also from the east coast. Because the postman had investigated the items, of course he had. Then again, the Mafia might have contacts everywhere, which only proved that his idea hadn't been that far-fetched after all.

The postman parked his van down by the barrier, then got out and opened the door at the back, where the parcel was ready and waiting, with the registered letter on top.

He had to hold it with both hands because it was bulky. The parcel measured seventy centimetres square or thereabouts and was barely twenty centimetres high. It was too heavy to be a lavatory seat, although that had been his first thought. He had a hunch that whatever was inside might be round. Square parcels usually had round contents.

He was particularly happy to pass the *No entry* sign. Well, that only applies to trespassers, he thought to himself. He was obviously free to enter, because he was bringing a registered letter. And a parcel.

He needed a signature.

And there was no way he was leaving the Head without it.

The postman took a right around the barrier and looked expectantly, albeit a little tensely, up at the house. If he was lucky, he would catch a glimpse of Maria Horder. He would love to know how she looked now.

He had managed two steps before someone called out.

'You there!' someone shouted behind him, and he stopped in his tracks. There was a note of aggression in the voice which he didn't like. When he turned around, he saw Jens Horder marching towards him. 'Where do you think you're going? Can't you read? I thought we had an agreement?'

The postman froze. He wasn't used to being spoken to like that. All right, so the Fuse made a habit of similarly belligerent outbursts – not to mention when she became physical. But Jens Horder had never raised his voice to anyone, certainly no one working for the post office.

'Of course, but . . .'

'Come here,' Horder snarled. 'What have you got for me?'

Reluctantly, the postman stepped back behind the barrier. He had time to feel cross with himself for not starting his round a little earlier; then he might have had an opportunity to chat to the wife, just the two of them. He was dying to know what was going on at the Horder place.

'I have a registered letter and a parcel,' he replied. 'They both need signing for. That's why I—'

He stopped himself when he caught a better look at Jens Horder. Horder was carrying seven or eight large plastic bags, stuffed to the brim. The sweat was trickling from his forehead, although it wasn't a particularly hot November day. And then there was his beard, and his clothes. It was a long time since the postman had seen Horder close up. The man looked dreadful.

'Why haven't you been down in your pickup, Horder? You usually are.'

'The pickup died. It's down on the south road. I had to leave it.'

'Gosh. That must have been a long walk home.'

'Give me the letter,' Horder demanded, setting down the bags. The postman caught a glimpse of something white in one of them. He carefully put the letter and the parcel on a tree stump next to the barrier and then offered Horder his receipt book and a pen. The recipient glared suspiciously at him before signing his name with an angry scrawl.

'By the way, who is M?' the postman asked, in his most ingratiating voice. He had no intention of letting this opportunity slip through his fingers. 'You regularly get

letters from them. And now a parcel as well. So I'm guessing that—'

'If that's all, then goodbye.' Jens Horder cut him off,
handing back the receipt book and the pen. The postman
had privately hoped that Horder would open the parcel
there and then.

'You don't want help with the parcel? I have a craft
knife on me . . .'

'So do I,' Jens Horder said, again with this inexplicable
coldness. Then he planted his hands on his hips and stared
at the postman with an expression it was difficult to inter-
pret as anything other than menacing.

'Well . . . goodbye then,' the postman said, and walked
back to his van. Jens Horder stayed put while the van
reversed. As the postman drove down the road towards
the Neck, he could still see Horder in his rear-view mir-
ror. He looked like a savage. A crazy savage.

Now, the postman wasn't by nature a judgemental man,
but he had long entertained a theory that Jens Horder had
done something to his mother, possibly even killed her.
Perhaps he was hiding her body in the big skip? The idea
would never have crossed his mind if it hadn't been for a
casual chat he had had one day with the ferry man in
Sønderby, in which he had learned that Else Horder never
took the ferry back to the mainland the previous Christmas. And if anyone was certain about anything, the ferry
man knew his passengers. However, he had been utterly
uninterested in the postman's suspicions. In fact, absolutely no one cared.

But then again, no one else had seen Jens Horder looking as he had looked down by the barrier. That was a man with something to hide. Otherwise, why the threatening behaviour?

What ultimately frustrated the postman more than anything, though, was that he didn't have any news to share with the others down at the pub, as he had hoped for. Although he had a snippet.

*M – Inventions for Life.*

But it was probably not enough for him to be taken seriously. Or even get anyone to listen. The others would invariably mutter that he should leave Horder alone to his grief. And that people were allowed to be a little eccentric.

# M

Jens Horder waited until the post van was out of sight. Then he turned his attention to the letter and the big parcel, which was balancing on the tree stump.

He started with the letter. It was in a padded buff-coloured envelope. As always, it contained an ordinary white envelope with cash inside. He looked at the white envelope, pulled it out and opened it. Business as usual, except this time the letter had been sent by registered post.

And this time a folded piece of paper had been slipped in alongside the white envelope.

He slowly pulled it out and felt immediately that it was thick with very fine grooves. When it reached the sunlight, it became ivory-coloured, and when he opened it he saw the watermark.

It was a commercial letterhead. And it wasn't just one sheet of paper, but two stapled together.

It was in his brother's handwriting.

*Dear Jens*

*There's no denying it has been a long time, and that's entirely my fault. For that reason, writing this letter isn't easy, but I hope that you will read it with an open mind.*

*I also hope that you can accept that I send you money every month. I send cash, as I assumed that was what you would prefer, and it's also more discreet. I would so hate to cause problems – even more than I imagine I caused back when I ran away from it all. I don't know if you can ever forgive me, but I hope so.*

*I'm sure you're doing well with the business, and you and the family have never needed my contributions, but I thought that it was the least I could do, given that I shirked my responsibility. I admit frankly that I also do it for my own sake. Yes, it's an attempt to make amends and ease my conscience. The latter hasn't been entirely successful.*

*I've never forgiven myself for leaving you in the lurch, but I just had to get out. As you probably sensed back then, I couldn't settle on the Head at all. I had terrible wanderlust and felt suffocated by the never-ending workload and the responsibility and, not least, Mum's expectations. Something about it all made me claustrophobic. We were so isolated, and there were so many other things that I wanted to do instead. I wanted to see the city, I wanted to invent. You wanted the trees.*

*You had also grown so quiet, Jens. I can't reproach you for that – I would never reproach you – because I knew that Dad's death hit you hard. But even so, I was secretly angry with you because I needed to talk to you. I missed you, even though we were together all the time. I couldn't bear it.*

*What happened was that one day I got talking to a holiday resident. He was an engineer from the mainland and very interested in my ideas. He was the one I spent time with when I was gone for hours. He offered me a job* with his company, but I said no initially, because I didn't think that I could leave you. And yet one day, I did just that. I had his business card in my pocket, but I didn't dare show it to you.

It was a really good job and the pay was great right from the start. At some point I set up my own business. We made lots of things in metal and steel, mostly filing systems, and so on. But my biggest success – brace yourself – were mechanical Christmas-tree stands. I made so much money that I travelled to Austria and set up a subsidiary down there.

During all that time I got a trusted employee back home to send money to the Head every month. She has done so faithfully, as far as I can gather. Now I'm back and engaged to that same trusted employee. We live in a wonderful apartment in town, but even so, we talk about moving. And starting a family. Fortunately, my fiancée is a little younger than me.

I must confess that I've started really missing my own family, you and Mum. I think about you often. It has just been so bloody difficult to contact you.

Once, I plucked up the courage and called the pub in Korsted. I think I spoke to the new owner – I'm guessing Oluf isn't there any more – or possibly a guest. Whoever he was, they were halfway through the New Year's Day lunch. I didn't tell him my name, I just asked general questions. I know how people like to talk and, as I said at the beginning, I didn't want to cause trouble for you. I learned that Else no longer lived on the Head but that she had visited you around Christmas and had apparently left again.

Sometime later I was at a dinner and happened to sit next to a lady who asked me about my surname. She told me that *she knew an Else Horder. It turned out that Mum had been staying with a friend of hers for a long time; she believed that they were cousins. Unfortunately, her friend had suffered terrible brain damage following a traffic accident, so the lady couldn't tell me where Mum was now, only that she definitely didn't live with her cousin any more.*

*But I'm guessing that you already know that, and that you also know where Mum lives today. Or is she back with you? You've always been good at handling Mum and her desire to control. I admire you for that.*

*Anyway, the best bit about my calling the pub was learning that you still lived on the Head – with your wife and your daughter. I'm absolutely delighted to learn that you are married and have a child, Jens. I do so hope that you're happy.*

*I would love to be a father myself. I started thinking about having a family much too late, I was far too busy inventing clever devices and manufacturing them. In one way, I wish I shared the love of nature which you and Dad had. There is something healthy about it, about you. Something real. Today, I miss working with wood, the fresh scent of the forest, and the sea, especially. In fact, I miss it so much that we're toying with the idea of moving to the island; if not the Head, then the main island. What would you say to that?*

*Initially, I would like to visit you and your family. Rekindle our relationship – that is, if you want to. Please would you write to me? Or call me, if that's an option. I've listed my home address and my phone number below.*

*Warm wishes*
*Your loving brother, Mogens*

*PS I'm sure that you grow the country's finest Christmas trees. And although you obviously prefer wood to metal and plastic, I wanted you to have one of the Christmas-tree stands my business manufactures. I'm taking the liberty of sending you a Christmas-tree stand as well as this letter.*

Jens Horder folded the letter once, then he folded it again before stuffing it into his inside pocket. He placed the envelope with the money in the front pocket of his coat. He briefly looked at the cumbersome parcel on the tree stump. Then he picked up the plastic bags and took a left around the barrier.

# The Man on the Head

Still staying in the forest, I tailed the man as he walked away from the dog. At one point he almost spotted me. He certainly looked in my direction for a long time. But I stood stock-still – I can do that – and in the end he moved on. He walked around the end of the building with the white room. It was strange to see someone walk that way rather than up the gravel road, and I wondered if he knew about the traps, but he couldn't possibly have done.

I think he was just lucky.

But I was scared because I didn't know what he wanted. Dad hadn't come back, and Mum was upstairs in the bedroom and couldn't do anything. And the man had seen the dog and the trap and taken my arrow. He was walking around with it in his hand. I was scared that he was looking for me. But he couldn't know that I was there. He hadn't seen me. Besides, I was dead.

When he reached the farmyard he stopped for a long time with his back to me. I'm sure he was staring at all the things. He probably wasn't used to seeing so many things gathered in one place, unless he also went to the junkyard.

I wish I knew what he wanted. I wanted Dad to come, yet at the same time I was scared about him turning up. Most of all, I just wanted the man to go away, I think. But without walking into a trap. And without bumping into Dad.

He just stood there at the edge of the yard with his back to the forest. I thought that he might make his way to the house, and I held my breath in case he walked past the silage harvester.

If you wanted to get from the white room to the house, you shouldn't pick the most obvious route, past the harvester. You should walk around the baker's pile first, in a zigzag pattern past the barn, then back towards the workshop, and then remember to take a right by the old cooker on the last stretch leading to the front door. I remembered it every single time – mostly because I'd never forgotten the look on Dad's face when he explained the route to me.

I didn't know exactly what it was about that cooker, but I had a hunch that it might tumble from the tall blocks it sat on if you went the wrong way round it.

Dad had made me promise to never ever do that. He trusted me more than any other person in the whole world, he said. It made me happy, but also a little bit sad. I don't really know why.

The man didn't go past the harvester. I think he heard a noise from the barn because he suddenly looked in that direction. Then he went around the farmyard and over to the barn door at the end. He stood there for a long time.

Meanwhile, I was wondering whether to shoot him.

I could easily hit him as he stood there, completely still, peering inside the barn. Especially if I crept a little closer and knelt down, because if I did that, I could hit anything I aimed at. By now I was as good an archer as Robin Hood.

But would Robin Hood ever shoot a man in the back? And would Mum even like me shooting a man at all?

And would Dad mind me *not* shooting him when I had the chance? I had a hunch that Dad would have shot him.

You would probably need several arrows and possibly also a club to whack him over the head to finish him off. I didn't know how killing a man would be compared to killing an animal or a granny, and what if I missed because I wasn't used to shooting men? I squeezed the bow in my hand.

And then the moment was gone because the man started walking around the barn. What was he doing in the field? No one but us ever went there, and we had stopped going. Had he come to take our chickens? I wasn't sure if we still had any. The geese were long gone.

I followed him. I had to leave my hideaway at the edge of the forest, but I made a quick dash from behind the trees to a new hideaway behind the pile with the yellow bicycle on it. From there I saw him wander along the field down to the end of our house. There were no traps around the back and I started to wonder if perhaps he knew about the traps after all.

He might see me if I followed him behind the barn, so I opted for the safe route across the farmyard instead. I could always find something to hide behind there. I was good at moving quickly and quietly, even when crawling.

He was knocking on the pantry door at the end of the house when I slipped behind the bathtub by the corner of the barn. I could hear it, and I caught a glimpse of him when he took a step back from the door. He was looking

271

for something. The key? A moment later I heard him let himself in and saw a rabbit run outside.

I waited.

Another two rabbits followed.

Then I heard his voice. 'Hello!' he shouted.

And then the kitchen curtain twitched. It was dark inside, so I couldn't see anything through the windowpane.

What if he found Mum?

If it hadn't been for Mum lying upstairs in the bedroom, I would have gone into hiding in the container at that point. Instead I crouched on the gravel behind the bathtub, staring up at Mum's dark window.

Then I heard an unexpected crash coming from inside the house and someone shouting. It couldn't be Mum. It was the man shouting.

No, he was screaming.

I don't think I thought anything at all. I just sat there, unable to move. Perhaps my tears couldn't move either, because I wanted to cry but I somehow couldn't. I couldn't make the tears come. And I couldn't make Carl come either. He didn't come. And neither did Dad.

And the man was still inside the house with Mum.

Any minute now he would come out of the back door. I had no idea what to do when that happened.

After a while – I don't know how long because it felt like a minute and an hour at the same time – the front door opened. I was so taken aback that I jumped. I hadn't expected to see him there. I had to turn slightly to get a better view.

Afterwards, I wondered whether I did it on purpose. Moving, I mean.

Whatever it was, he spotted me. I'll never forget it. 'Oi, you!' he called out. It was the first time in ages that someone other than Dad had spoken to me.

Perhaps I should have grabbed an arrow and fired my bow from behind the bathtub. I could have shot him through the heart, I'm sure of it. He was standing at the top of the steps, it would have been easy peasy.

But deep down I didn't want to. When your own heart is beating so loud you can hear it, you don't want to aim at anything. Especially not another heart.

So I did something else. I ran.

I picked a safe route along the barn, then dashed in a semicircle to the right towards the place in the forest I had come from. He would never catch me in the thicket and I had a head start. But although I knew that he couldn't catch me, I felt all mixed up and I didn't run as fast as I could have.

It felt as if my heart was trying to pound its way out of my chest. And, at the same time, it was as if someone was beating it from the outside. As if someone were trying to bash it back inside me. Or bash me back? Perhaps it was Carl.

I stopped and looked for the man once I was some way towards the forest. He was running towards me and seemed to have chosen the safe route around the pile with the cooker on it. He shouted something, but I couldn't hear what it was.

All I could think about was that he was making a

beeline for me – and that very soon he would reach the silage harvester.

I wanted to run on, but I couldn't.

The next moment I saw the man being knocked over and yanked violently up into the air, so that he ended up dangling from the harvester.

Head down.

Just like in Sherwood Forest, I thought.

His foot was caught in a noose. The other was kicking wildly out into the air, and his arms were flailing, as if he was trying to touch the ground, which was just out of his reach. The dog lead he had had around his neck fell off and settled underneath him, while he spun on his own axis.

He looked a bit like a fish on a line.

'Get me down from here!' he shouted.

I didn't know what to do.

I waited for a long time. He continued to shout, and I continued to stand there. Stock-still. I could do that.

Eventually he stopped thrashing his arms about and the anger left his voice. He just hung there, rotating slowly like the violin over the wood-burning stove used to do. And the Christmas tree in the ceiling, if you nudged it a bit.

He kept on talking to me, and I kept on not replying.

'Please help me get down.'

'I won't hurt you. I just want to talk to you.'

'You can't leave me hanging here.'

Like that.

I didn't budge.

'I spoke to the woman in the bedroom. Are you two related? She asked me to help you.'

At that point I may have twitched ever so slightly.

'Help us?' I said after a while. I could see that he couldn't hear me, so I walked a little closer.

'Help us?' I asked him again.

He nodded, which actually looked quite funny because he was upside down and turning around. He started rotating gently the other way.

When he was face to face with me again he narrowed his eyes.

'Are you a girl?' he asked me.

I nodded.

'Did you shoot the dog?' he said then, and my heart crept all the way up into my mouth. I tried nodding and shaking my head at the same time.

'Yes, but it wasn't me who—'

And it was at that moment that Dad appeared in the farmyard. He looked at us. Then he set down all his plastic bags and walked slowly towards us, using the safe route along the workshop. I saw his head glide across the piles, and in between I could also see his whole body. He carried on staring, but I couldn't tell whether he was staring at me.

A man was hanging upside down between us. Perhaps he was staring at him.

★

Dad told me to make space in the white room. I had to clear a passage to the bed Dad usually slept in, the one where my granny was killed. Dad had already moved the heaviest things.

I did as I was told without knowing why. But I was scared. Scared about what would happen to the man, and scared about what would happen to us.

Just as I had pushed the last bag blocking the way aside, the man appeared in the door. The room was dim, and he had the midday sun in his back, so I couldn't see him clearly at first. But I could see that it was him because he was bigger than Dad and, when he took a step forwards, I could also see that he had something tied around his face. It looked like a big sausage made from cloth had been squashed into his mouth.

He didn't make a sound.

I didn't make a sound.

Then I noticed that Dad was standing behind him. He told the man to lie down on the bed. I pressed my back against a box as he came closer. He looked at me, and I looked away.

When he turned towards the bed I saw that his hands were tied behind his back. I could also see the knife in Dad's hand. It was the same knife which had once cut into my baby sister.

Something in me wanted the man to have evil eyes. But his eyes weren't evil, not now, and not when he had been dangling from the harvester. I couldn't help thinking about the dog and the trap, and how the man had wept when he saw his dog. Evil eyes don't cry, do they?

Dad tied him to the four bedposts. One of the man's trouser legs had been pushed up slightly, and I spotted a red groove around his ankle, just above his sock. It cut deep into his flesh and it was also bleeding a little. My stomach churned at the sight. It must have really hurt hanging from the harvester. It must really hurt now.

And that was when I realized how much all the rabbits in all those snares must have hurt, if the dark hadn't been able to take their pain away. I had freed lots of dead rabbits from lots of thin snares and seen how the string had cut deep into their fur and flesh. What if they hadn't died straightaway? What if they felt the wire carve itself deeper and deeper into them and the darkness had never taken away their pain?

I watched the man's eyes carefully. When they looked at Dad, they looked scared. When they looked at me, the man looked like the dog when it pleaded for help.

Dad turned to me.

'Stay here and keep an eye on him, Liv. But from a distance. Fetch me if he tries to escape.' Then he made his way towards the door. 'We'll need him later.'

'Where are you going?' I asked anxiously. I didn't want to be alone with the man. Carl being there, on and off, didn't really count.

'I've got things to do in the workshop. I'll leave the door open,' Dad said from the doorway.

'Please may I go and see Mum?'

'No. I want you to stay here. Your mum needs to be alone.'

Then he left.

How could you need to be alone?

\*

I watched the man from the doorway. I had my dagger in my belt. My bow and my quiver of arrows were ready right outside the door. I had placed them there, next to the camping stove, when I moved things around in the white room.

The man just lay there.

He tried speaking through the fabric sausage, but only managed strange noises, which I couldn't understand. So he stopped. I thought it might be nice if he could write things down instead, but it would have meant me freeing one of his hands, and I didn't know whether he was right-handed or left-handed. I didn't want to risk untying them both.

I was left-handed, we had discovered, Mum and I. She was right-handed, but she said that either was fine. In order to prove it, she would sometimes write with her left, always capitals. Perhaps the man could also write with either, so it wouldn't matter which hand I freed. But in any case I would still need something he could write with and on, and that was upstairs with Mum. And I wasn't allowed up there. Then I remembered that Dad didn't want me to loosen anything at all.

I knew that I wasn't supposed to untie the man. But Carl had turned up, and he wanted to.

He kept pestering me.

All at once, I burst into tears. The man looked at me and made a noise. He flapped the fingers on his right hand.

I stared at them and cried even harder.

Then I went to the workshop.

*

Dad was also crying.

He was sitting on the edge of the big coffin; the plastic bags he had brought back lay scattered around him. Some gauze had rolled out of one of them. There were canisters of oil over by the workbench, and behind them three sacks of salt.

He didn't scream or howl. He sobbed quietly, just like I used to. The tears trickled into his beard, and I thought that his beard must be very heavy and wet.

When he saw me he reached out his hand to me. He had nice eyes. Evil eyes can't cry.

Slowly, I walked up to him. Finally, I was near enough that his hand could grab my sleeve. He pulled me close and put his arm around me. I stood sideways between his legs, and his giant wet beard tickled my neck.

We both cried. I'm not quite sure why I cried, but perhaps it was mostly because I didn't know why he was crying.

His hand felt warm and nice through my sweater. It was a long time since he had held me like that. I guess that was another reason I was crying. Or perhaps it was because of the coffin.

'There's something we have to do,' he suddenly whispered.

I stood very still behind his hand.

'I have to help your mum, Liv.'

I said nothing.

'We want her to be OK, don't we?'

I nodded and looked right ahead. At the workbench. I could see the sacks of salt and the oil canisters.

'And we want her to stay here with us. We want to keep her. Don't we, Liv?'

I nodded again. Tentatively. I really did want to keep Mum, but I wasn't sure that now was a good time to nod.

'I'm scared that we'll lose her if we don't do something. And we're the only ones who can.'

'Help her?' I asked.

'Yes. Help her.'

'What about the man?'

'He can't help her. But he can help us help her.'

That made no sense to me.

I realized that we had stopped crying. My neck felt thick on the inside and wet on the outside . . . where his beard had brushed it.

'But how . . . ?'

It took a while before he replied.

'She's still not . . . small enough . . . for us to get her through the door. I think it's better that we do it upstairs. Then she can lie there with all her books. That would be nice, don't you think?'

I nodded again.

'And dry out?' I asked cautiously, staring at the sacks.

'Yes.'

'And grow smaller?'

'Yes, exactly.'

'For some weeks. Until you can . . .'

'Yes. You'll have to help me clean the resin. And I think we need to fetch the big glass jars from the chemist's outhouse. I think they're by the baker's pile. But we have plenty of time, Liv. We have all the time in world. She needs her bath first, her salt bath.'

'But what about the man?'

'He can help me carry the bathtub upstairs. I can't carry it on my own, and although you're very strong you're not strong enough. So, in a way, it was a stroke of luck that he turned up. I had been wondering how I would . . .'

Then he stopped talking.

'But what about the man? Afterwards? Will he leave then?'

Dad hesitated, then he said: 'Yes, he'll leave afterwards.' His voice sounded strange.

'Then he had better watch out for the traps along the gravel road,' I said.

'Yes.'

'Perhaps I could show him where they are?'

'Yes . . . you may.'

I could see that he wanted to add something.

'Do you know why he came, Liv?'

'Yes, he was looking for his dog . . . down by . . .'

Suddenly my throat tightened. There was something I had to ask Dad. Something about the dog and the trap which had bit deep into its leg, making it scream and howl. Something about the trap with the horrible teeth.

I couldn't.

I started to cry again.

'And he was alone?'

I nodded. The tears poured out of me like two small waterfalls that kept on running.

Dad pulled me close.

'Don't be sad. Your mum won't feel a thing. I have some pills for her. They'll take away all her pain at once. It'll be quick and she'll feel so much better afterwards. I think she needs it.'

He had also said that she needed to be alone.

I didn't want Mum to be alone. I wanted to be with Mum.

'But then she'll be all alone?'

'No, once she's ready, she'll be down here with us. She won't be crying, and she won't be ill or hungry, and she'll never be in pain again. You'll still be able to read to her, and do you know something, Liv . . .'

He stroked my hair.

'. . . she'll be able to hear you, because she'll still have her heart.'

He reached his hand into the coffin and pulled something out. 'And we'll be able to see her.'

I stared at the most beautiful drawing ever drawn of a human being. I stared at Mum. She was smiling.

Dad got up without warning and I took a step back. I couldn't work out what to do. I couldn't cry. Carl hovered nervously by the door. I could tell he wanted to run away.

Dad looked bigger than ever.

He had drawn the picture.

And he had made the trap.

And now we were about to kill Mum.

'Come on, Liv,' he said, and I followed him, without wanting to.

First we went back to the man in the white room. He lay very still with his legs and arms stretched out and his mouth gagged. The ropes from his wrists and ankles to the bedposts were taut. When Dad entered, he raised his head slightly and looked at us.

Dad just glanced at him, then pulled me outside. He closed the door behind him.

'You wait here and keep guard, Liv. He can't escape, but you keep guard and use your bow, if necessary. I'll go over to the house and move some things out of the way so we can bring in the tub.'

'I want to talk to Mum,' I whispered through the beginning of tears.

Dad bent down and looked me in the eye. His face was so close to mine that I could feel his beard and the brim of his cap.

His eyes hung right in front of mine like hard, black stones. They were no longer crying. They weren't even shiny. They weren't Dad's eyes. They were stones.

'*No*,' he said. 'You stay here. I'll be back in a minute.'

I don't know how long he was gone. I only know that the sun had reached the chimney on the house. There were no clouds at all. The sky was big and blue.

# Pupating

The glow from the candlelight didn't reach Jens Horder's eyes when he showed her the pills. In his other hand he held a glass of water.

Maria saw only his hands. They were shaking.

She nodded and slowly opened her mouth. The corners of her mouth were cracked. She was thirsty and tired.

For a moment she felt his lips on her forehead.

Quivering like a butterfly.

Then he disappeared back into the darkness. She heard his footsteps down the stairs. The sound of heavy objects being dragged across the floor below. Him groaning.

Perhaps he was crying.

Then she found the notepad by her side.

And her very last bit of strength.

I THINK THAT'S IT

# The Captive

The gag cut into the corners of his mouth, and Roald had to breathe deeply through his nose to keep the nausea at bay. The fact that the air in the room was so suffocating didn't help either. He had to stay focused. He had to ignore the smell and value the oxygen which, after all, it still contained. If he didn't concentrate, his fear of choking would overpower him. Throwing up would be the end of him. If the cold he had only recently got rid of crept up on him now and blocked his nose, that would also be the end of him. What about sneezing? Was it possible to sneeze when you had a gag pressed into the back of your mouth? Surely the sneeze would explode in his throat and choke him? He had to keep reminding himself about the oxygen. There was oxygen in the air and free passage through his nose. He breathed deeply and tried getting his pulse down. And he tried to think.

NEED HELP ALL 3, Maria had written.

You could say that again.

Roald was worried about her and the girl, but at this moment in time he was mostly concerned about Jens Horder. Exactly how far gone was he? Was he capable of murder?

And what had he meant when he said: 'We'll need him later?' Then again, it gave Roald a faint hope that he wasn't about to be killed, at least not immediately. On the other hand, *Need him?*

Need him for what?

Roald thought about the people of Korsted. Had anyone known about his walk to the Head? No, he hadn't mentioned it to anyone. Why on earth hadn't he told someone, spoken to the police officer, left a note for the chef?

If he didn't come back today, then what? When would people start to notice? At some point Short Fuse's Lars would start to wonder why Roald hadn't returned his dog. He would ring the pub later tonight. Perhaps even walk down there, if he could be bothered. He probably couldn't, and his explosive wife undoubtedly had jobs that she wanted him to do. So Lars wouldn't do anything until tomorrow, which was when he would bump into the chef, who would be back by then and who would also be wondering about Roald's absence.

And at that point they would contact the police. Not until then. Not until tomorrow. And probably not until late in the day. To act quickly would be regarded as jumping the gun.

Roald focused on his breathing. Jens Horder would bloody well have to let him go. There had to be limits to his madness.

Nevertheless, the family was in desperate need of help. All three of them. Roald made up his mind to be as accommodating as possible. He would signal to them that he meant them no harm at all. That he was no threat.

That would probably fix it.

And that was when the penny dropped.

In the midst of all the junk and his terror and confusion over the boy, who was a girl, he hadn't processed that Jens Horder had referred to her as Liv. Liv Horder. She was the daughter they had reported dead.

And now her father knew that he had been found out.

At that moment Jens Horder appeared in the doorway. Roald's pulse rocketed again. Need him for what? And what would happen to him afterwards?

'I'm going to untie you now,' Horder said, squatting down by one of the bedposts.

The pain shot through Roald when the rope briefly tightened even more around his ankle, which was already hurting after the encounter with the silage harvester. Then the rope slackened and he felt the blood return to his foot. He moved it carefully to avoid cramping. Soon his other foot was free.

Before Horder started untying his hands he pulled out his knife and showed it to Roald. 'Don't try anything stupid,' he said, placing the knife on the bed, well out of Roald's reach.

Roald decided not to try anything stupid.

Horder's voice was cold, but Roald could feel the heat radiating from him and see the beads of sweat on his forehead. His gaze also seemed cold and distant, and yet his eyes were swollen and red . . . as if he had just been crying.

The girl appeared in the doorway. Roald could see the top of her quiver of arrows behind one of her shoulders and the bow in her hand. Jens Horder looked behind and glanced at her before turning his attention back to Roald.

'My daughter is a formidable archer. Make no mistake. I've ordered her to shoot you if you try anything. And believe me: she won't miss.'

Roald believed him. All his limbs were finally free, but he stayed on his back where he was. He still couldn't speak because of the gag. Should he try to remove it now that he could use his hands again?

Horder picked up the knife and positioned himself in front of Roald.

Roald pointed cautiously at his mouth and the scarf or whatever it was he had been made to bite on for so long. It tasted and smelled like a mixture of wool and cowshed. Horder looked as if he didn't know whether or not to give him permission to remove it.

Roald faked a cough.

'Please take it out, Dad,' the girl pleaded anxiously over by the door, and Roald immediately coughed a little harder. Only this time he genuinely started to choke. His hands reached instinctively for the fabric, trying to pull it down. It was too tight for him to take it off. Tears welled up in his eyes.

Horder appeared to realize from the expression in Roald's eyes that this was serious because he quickly grabbed the knot behind Roald's head and untied it. Then he threw the scarf on to a pile next to the bed.

Roald coughed and gasped for air until he was able to breathe again with relative ease.

'Thank you,' he said after a while.

'You'll do exactly as I say, understand?' Jens Horder said, holding the knife perilously close to one of Roald's wrists.

'Yes.'

'Good. I need your help. The two of us will carry a bathtub up to the first floor of the main house.'

'A bathtub?' It was pretty much the last thing Roald had expected to hear.

'Yes, my wife needs a bath. Come on, get up.'

Roald was herded along a specific route across the farmyard to the bathtub, the one that Liv had tried to hide behind. It was the free-standing sort. With feet.

Only it wasn't the kind of bathtub you would want to take a bath in. Yellow blotches and tidemarks of dark grime had settled on the enamel sides and on the bottom. A woodland snail was floating around a dried lake of spruce needles and hose clamps. Jens Horder used his shabby cap to empty the tub with a couple of sweeping movements. Afterwards, he put the cap back on.

The bathtub was as heavy as sin. Roald was ordered to walk in front, and even before he reached the steps leading up to the front door he was dripping with sweat. He understood why Jens Horder had taken off his coat and chucked it over a barrel somewhere.

The archer followed them like a shadow. There was no doubt that she understood her role. She never once took her eyes off him. Roald felt conflicted at being threatened by a scruffy little kid, but the threat seemed real enough. Besides, he had already seen what her arrows could do. They were not toys.

Liv opened the door for them and was told to wait outside in the farmyard. With her bow at the ready.

Roald had already concluded that they couldn't possibly get the bathtub through the hall and up to the first floor. Although it might be the most direct route through the house, it was piled high with stuff. However, when he entered the darkness and the stench he realized what it was that had caused Horder to sweat earlier. Things had been pushed aside and rearranged to create a slightly wider passageway. It might actually be possible to get the bathtub up to the first floor now.

It was completely absurd. She was dying up there. The woman didn't need a bath. She needed help.

It wasn't easy. It wasn't easy in any sense of the word. Roald had never carried anything so heavy, but his body had apparently accepted that there was no escape and found strength in his fear.

The trickiest part was to angle the bathtub correctly so that they could get it into the bedroom, but Jens Horder had worked out exactly how it should be done. Then again, with all the things he had dragged into the house, he had by now accumulated a lot of experience in negotiating doorways.

He had made room along the bed, or at least there wasn't as much junk as before. The bucket had gone, thank God, but the smell was still intolerable.

Roald glanced at the huge woman still lying buried by her own body and the stuff on the bed. The candle flickered on the bedside table, and he didn't have time to catch her eye. However, he did notice that the duvet had been rearranged. It looked almost as if she had been lovingly tucked in, like when you tuck in a child.

An unemotional Jens Horder instructed him how to navigate the bathtub in. It had to be closely aligned with the bed. Why? So they could roll her into it? Roald feared that the poor woman was so big she might easily get stuck in the tub. How on earth would they ever get her out of there? He was, however, quite certain that now was not the time to voice his concerns.

Especially when he sneaked a peek at Maria's face and saw that she was dead.

She had to be dead. You didn't lie like that with staring eyes and your mouth half open unless you were dead.

She seemed to be smiling faintly.

He quickly looked away and caught a glimpse of a large glass of pills which looked far too empty. Had she swallowed them by choice? Or . . . ?

'One of the feet is caught by something in your corner. You need to move it,' came the order from the other end of the bathtub.

Roald obediently squatted down next to the headboard to free the bathtub foot. He moved a book that was lying on the floor, along with a small, empty notebook with frayed bits of paper in the spiral binding, and then tried to pick up a woollen blanket which had half fallen off the bed and was also in the way. He had to tug hard to get the blanket out from underneath the swaddled human being, and the movement caused Maria's left hand to suddenly appear from under the duvet. Roald froze at the sight of her open palm. A ballpoint pen was trapped in a deep fold of skin.

He glanced furtively at Jens Horder, who was standing with his back to him over by the door, then placed two fingers on Maria's wrist. No, there was no pulse. Roald gently pushed her hand back under the duvet.

And that was when he noticed it. Something was tucked in between the mattress and the bedframe, right where the woollen blanket had been. It was a slim green file. He glanced towards the door again. Jens Horder was busy moving a big cardboard box that perched precariously on top of some other boxes and which Roald had accidentally bumped into with the bathtub.

Roald carefully pulled out the file. 'To Liv', it said in cursive writing on the cover. He opened it, only for a moment, but long enough to see that it contained both handwritten letters and several smaller notes, some apparently stuffed randomly into the file. A single scrap of paper from a notebook seemed to have escaped and was still trapped between the mattress and the bedframe. He could barely make out what it said because it was written with clumsy capitals on top of one another.

He didn't have time to think about why he did it. Quick as lightning, he stuffed the loose scrap into the file with the other notes, then slipped the file under his shirt. He could feel his heart pounding furiously.

He continued to squat behind the bathtub for a few more seconds while he tried to calm his nerves. Then he got up and pushed the tub close to the bed, just like he had been told to. Jens Horder was still facing away from him. The knife was tucked into his belt at the back.

If only he could slip past him, but how? He looked at the woman in the bed for a moment and then he said:

'I think your wife is trying to say something.'

Jens Horder spun around and stared at Maria. Seconds later, he was back by the headboard.

Roald stepped aside to make way for him.

'She was trying to say something just now,' he lied again.

Horder stroked the dead woman's hand and moved his face close to her.

'My darling,' he whispered. 'Are you still awake?'

And that was when Roald ran. He jumped past the bath-tub on his way to the door. The box which Horder had struggled with was still close to the edge of the pile it was resting on, and with his newly acquired strength Roald managed to pull it down behind him. It hit the floor with a crash and something shattered. Out in the passage, he knocked down everything he could in order to block Jens Horder's path. Some big clip frames landed cooperatively across the floor of the corridor. A standard lamp keeled over, dragging rolls of fabric with it. A flower-pot stand was knocked over and bumped down the stairs, along with engine parts and tinned food, petrol cans and toys. Something hit a crumbling sack, which responded by spewing its foul-smelling contents over the landing.

Roald made it down the stairs and out through the hall. He didn't look back. He tore open the heavy front door, just as he had done earlier but experiencing a different fear this time. The fear of death was chasing him, as were the smell, the noises and the darkness. As soon as he was outside he slammed the door shut behind him.

The light was overwhelming, but not blinding. The sun threw itself into the farmyard from the south-west. It was on his side. And a sunbeam revealed a kneeling archer who was aiming her bow at him.

Roald ran down the steps, towards the child and the bow. 'Don't shoot, Liv!' he called out. 'I promised your mum to help you, and I've got something—'

He slowed his pace when the child suddenly stood up and pointed. '*Stop!*' she screamed. 'Go the other way around the cooker.'

Roald reacted instinctively. He screeched to a halt and took a step back to run the other way around the pile with the old cooker on the top. A second later the cooker crashed on to the path with a mighty bang.

The girl tossed aside her bow and clutched her head with both hands.

Roald's heart was in his throat as he ran towards her. *That poor child*, was the only thought going through his mind. *That poor, poor child.*

She slumped to her knees as he came closer. And that was when he realized that she wasn't staring at him. But at something behind him.

# Inferno

Roald turned around to see what Liv was looking at. It wasn't, as he had initially feared, Jens Horder emerging from the front door, brandishing a knife.

It was Jens Horder's house giving up.

First the roof ridge sunk down, as if the house were taking its last breath. Then the entire building exhaled in a deafening sigh. It crumbled. Everything seemed to fall inwards – with the exception of the front door, which was flung across the farmyard.

Roald held the child in a tight grip when he saw a red glow through the first-floor window. The flames were quick to follow. Soon the ground floor was also engulfed in fire.

The child wept quietly but pitifully amidst the noise. Roald squatted down behind her with his arms around her sobbing body and his head on her frail shoulders. The soft feathers on the arrows tickled his throat.

'My mum,' he heard her say. 'And my dad.'

'Your mum was already dead when we got up there,' he said, as gently as possible. 'She died in her sleep. She didn't feel a thing. And your dad was with her. The last thing I saw was him kissing her.'

Roald briefly considered whether he had a duty to try to rescue Jens Horder from the burning house, however small the chance, but it was an inferno of flames and smoke. No one would get out of there alive.

'It all happened so quickly,' he said then. 'Your dad didn't feel a thing either.'

'Good,' the girl sobbed.

Roald carefully but firmly turned her around so that she was facing him, and then lifted her to standing. He placed his hands on her shoulders.

'You and I are going to go now,' he said. 'I'll take care of you, but we have to leave now. The fire will spread soon.'

The girl nodded again and picked up her bow. As she stood there with the quiver of arrows on her back and the bow in her hand, she resembled a small, brave soldier.

She looked up at him. Roald didn't know what to say next. Her eyes were filled with tears, but she was subjecting him to the most intense scrutiny he had ever experienced. She examined his eyes, searching for something. He wasn't even aware that he was also crying until he felt the tears roll down his cheek.

Then she looked like she had come to some sort of conclusion, because she put down the bow, resolutely lifted the strap of the quiver over her head and chucked her ammunition down beside her weapon without giving it a second glance. The soldier's acceptance that the war was over.

'Good, then let's—' Roald said, but he was interrupted.

'There are traps, so *don't* follow me,' the girl ordered him, with admirable resolve in her little voice. 'I'll be back in two secs. Stay here.'

Before Roald had time to protest, the brown-and-orange

sweater disappeared through the piles, using God knows what route, but she was heading for the barn.

He sized up the house again. They probably had some time, but not much. The heat pressed against him and his eyes began to sting.

He spotted Jens Horder's coat thrown over a barrel in a nearby pile. Roald picked it up. It was heavy and falling apart. The suede had been worn shiny and the lining was fraying in several places. In one of the big front pockets was a thick buff-coloured envelope. Roald stuffed it into his own front pocket and quickly examined the rest of Horder's coat, while looking out anxiously for Liv.

In the inside pocket was a folded letter.

Roald hesitated. He had always respected the confidentiality of other people's letters and had never read as much as a postcard which wasn't addressed to him. But then again, this situation was rather . . .

He unfolded the letter and started to read.

*Dear Jens*

*There's no denying it has been a long time, and that's entirely my fault. For that reason, writing this letter isn't easy . . .*

When at that very second Liv came running from the barn, he quickly folded the letter and stuffed it into his inside pocket. Behind the girl he saw the clapped-out dapple-grey horse and some smaller shadows disappear in the direction of the forest.

'Come on!' she called out as she ran past him. Roald

forgot about Horder's coat and followed her across the farmyard, zigzagging between the heaps. He looked back towards the parts of the house where the fire had yet to spread, but it was only a matter of time before flying sparks would reach the piles of junk and the other buildings.

It was an odd sort of fire. There was howling and hissing from the house and a deep rumble underneath it all. At the same time, thick, dark smoke crept around the building, as if guarding it. Above this scene, however, the sky was bright and blue, ignorant of the pain below. As if the drama didn't interest it, as if it couldn't be bothered with the smoke. It seemed simply to have withdrawn from all of it and be waiting patiently for a time when it could spread out again.

'Wait there!' Liv called out again, and Roald obeyed her orders instinctively. He understood that the child was in charge now. He had come to save her, but the truth was that she would be the one to get them out of here safely. He looked at the old silage harvester. Somehow, he had always believed that contraption to be the least terrifying of all agricultural machinery; it reminded him of a good-natured herbivore from the dawn of time. Now he was sure that he could never see a silage harvester as anything other than a monster ever again.

He watched her run through a door in the wooden building. It must lead to the workshop people had spoken about. He called out to her, knowing full well that she couldn't hear him. They really had to leave. For God's sake. He would have to go and get her.

Then suddenly she reappeared. 'I've got it,' she called out. 'Come on.'

Roald ran as if pulled by an invisible string. She was holding something in her hand, a small clip frame, he believed, and another item, smaller and different, but he couldn't see what it was.

She ran down towards the gravel road but stayed frighteningly close to the fire.

'Don't you think we had better go the other way round?' he called out anxiously, but he continued to follow the child. She made no reply, merely beckoned him on.

'Run to the end of the workshop and stay close to it,' she called out now, doing so herself. He copied her and ran right behind her, with his hand on the cladding. He noticed that she was still armed. A dagger was dangling from a leather sheath in her belt, slapping lightly against her thigh.

He looked back. The fire had reached a tree near the house where flames stuck out of a small gable window like orange tongues. Some roof tiles fell on to the gravel, and without warning a huge spruce branch swept across the road with enormous force. Roald bellowed in terror as the branch passed him at chest height. It had to be a trap, and if he hadn't followed Liv's orders, the branch would have knocked him clean off his feet. He couldn't get out of this place fast enough.

And so Roald nearly cried out in despair when the girl didn't continue down the road which would lead them away but stopped at the big skip.

'I won't be long,' she shouted out to him. 'Hold this.'

She handed him a small drawing in an old frame. And an hourglass. An hourglass.

Then she ran alongside the skip and scaled a couple of boxes and a tractor tyre before reaching the furthest hatch.

'Liv, please stop. No more . . . We have to get out of here.'

But she had already disappeared inside, having opened the hatch as if she had done it every day of her life. Roald stared after her, speechless, before looking nervously at the buildings.

The fire had yet to reach a section of the farmyard between the gable end of the burning house and the dark wooden workshop. The old spinning wheel leaning against the wall below the kitchen window had got a new lease of life. The wheel spun while the flames danced underneath it. The fire had also reached the pile which had had the cooker at the top. On the first floor flames were coming out of every window.

It occurred to Roald that he was staring at a home with two burning parents inside it while waiting for their young daughter to emerge from what amounted to a skip. Her whole world, everything she had ever known, was going up in flames.

None of this felt real.

He looked at the framed drawing. It was a portrait of a woman, a beautiful woman. Perhaps it was Maria? It had her mouth. He was reminded of the *Mona Lisa*. This drawing was signed with a discreet 'Jens' in the right-hand corner. Roald stuffed both the portrait and the hourglass into one of the big front pockets of his coat. Then he reached for the letter in his inside pocket and quickly unfolded it. His gaze skimmed the pages without taking anything in. It was not until the final lines that he managed to hook his attention into the text:

*Initially, I would like to visit you and your family. Rekindle our relationship – that is, if you want to. Please would you write to me? Or call me, if that's an option. I've listed my home address and my phone number below.*

*Warm wishes*
*Your loving brother, Mogens*

There was a PS, which he didn't have time to read because at that moment the hatch of the skip slammed shut. He could feel the metal echo from where he was standing.

Roald folded the letter and returned it to his pocket as he watched the girl come towards him. She had a book in one hand and a teddy bear in the other. A teddy bear.

She was still a child, just a child. A brave little child, armed with a dagger and a teddy bear. And now it was his job to take care of her.

When she reached him Roald tentatively stuck out his hand to her. She stared at it for a moment. Then she tucked the teddy under her left arm, freeing one hand. It cautiously took Roald's.

'Can we run now?' he asked. 'Down to the Neck?'

She nodded. 'Yes, but we need to avoid another two traps.'

'OK. You lead the way.'

She nodded again, and they ran.

His footsteps sounded like heavy explosions in the gravel. Hers made no sound. She ran so silently that he had to look down to see if her feet really touched the ground. She guided him away from the road and around the tall spruces, then back on to the road, then she led him right around the barrier, which they had to sidle past. Her small hand had a firm grip on his now. He felt strangely safe.

On the other side of the barrier they stopped, as if by prior agreement. As if the barrier were a protective device that could stop flames, death and tragedy. As if they were safe now.

'Any more traps?' Roald asked his well-informed guide.

She shook her head and stared up at her burning home. The fire had reached the workshop now. The big skip lay in front of it like a long shadow, awaiting its fate. Several of the trees were ablaze, and around them small fires were burning in the grass.

It broke Roald's heart to imagine the girl's feelings at the sight.

'What's your book about?' he asked.

'It's *Robin Hood*,' she replied, looking down at it.

'Would you like me to carry it for you?'

She nodded and gave him the book, and he found room for it in one of his coat pockets. Under his vest and the lining of his trousers he could feel the green file sticking to his stomach.

'You shot the dog through the heart so that it wouldn't suffer, didn't you?'

She nodded again, and looked sadly at him.

'It was a fine shot. And the kind thing to do. Thank you.'

Her small face lit up briefly, although the tears were streaming down her cheeks now.

'I can understand why you're crying,' Roald whispered.

And then he noticed that Liv was still clutching something in the hand which had held the book.

'Is there anything else you would like me to hold for you?'

She carefully unclenched her fist and showed him a small piece of amber. 'It's my dad's. There's an old ant inside it.'

'Really,' Roald said. 'Let's take a look at it when we get back to my house.'

She nodded and put the amber into his pocket herself.

'Would you like to carry on holding your teddy?'

'Yes,' she whispered, pressing the teddy bear to her chest.

He spotted the parcel lying on the tree stump. 'That parcel . . . Do you know what's inside?'

Liv shook her head.

'Shall we take it with us?' Roald looked anxiously at the fire eating its way towards them. He shouldn't have asked. They needed to leave now.

'No,' Liv said, looking back up towards the burning house. 'I want to get away from here.'

She grabbed his hand. And they ran.

They followed the sharp bend to the south and ran down the gravel road along the spruces, through the birch grove, over the small clearing and onwards past the low-growing pines and the large area of wild roses, which were well past flowering for this year. Eventually they reached the Neck. Roald was starting to feel an unaccustomed lightness. His feet danced underneath him in an even rhythm, and her noiseless steps flew past him like a steady pulse in double time.

When they were almost at the bottom of the Neck they stopped and turned around. A thick black plume of smoke rose from the middle of the Head, and they could see a red glow behind the southernmost trees. Perhaps all of the Head would burn. Perhaps it was the right thing.

Roald placed his hands on the girl's shoulders. He could hear her breathing and feel her shoulders rise and fall, so she wasn't wholly supernatural. She could fly, but she was still breathing.

'I believe that you have a nice uncle and that we need to find him. But I'll look after you whatever happens, so don't you worry.'

'I'm not worried,' she said. 'Are you?' She tilted her head and looked up at him.

He stroked her hair.

'No. Not any more.'

'What's your name?'

'Roald.'

'My name is Liv. And I'm not dead.'

'I know that.' He smiled.

'Where do you live?'

'Down at the pub.'

'I've been there.'

# Things Take Time

The lady with the white name badge says it'll take time. She has read everything Mum wrote to me. We've a lot to talk about, she says.

She says that I haven't learned things which other children my age have learned. However, I can do some things which they can't, and I've seen someone get killed.

She says that my life has been turned upside down. I don't really get what that's supposed to mean. It's to do with me being neither a child nor a grown-up; that sometimes I think like a child and sometimes I think like an adult, and every now and then I do things which *no one* ought to do. I think they mean to teach me how to think and what to do.

I'm not allowed to lock the door to my room or barricade it. But it's OK for me to still snap and shake my biscuits, and it's really good that I write down my thoughts. I'm also allowed to repeat myself. The lady says I'm very good at writing and speaking, and that it doesn't matter at all if time and things get muddled up a bit.

When I asked her if it's also OK that people get muddled up, she looked at me strangely and nodded. But she didn't understand. I don't think I'm going to tell her everything.

She also says that it's not my fault.

I already know that.

\*

Sometimes I dream about Dad. It's the same dream every time. He's standing in the doorway of our burning house, and he has an arrow through his heart. I know that it's my arrow, my best arrow. I also know that he's dying.

But he doesn't fall down immediately. He takes a few steps towards me before he lies down in the gravel in front of me. His hair and beard are as wild as ever before, but when his cap falls off I see that he has started to go bald. His movements are slow, and he seems very calm. Just like the stag in the moonlight. I'm sure that he's looking into my eyes and that he's not angry with me. It wasn't my fault.

Then he closes his eyes.

And then I wake up.

In one way it's a good dream, although it makes me cry. Perhaps I'll tell it to the lady one day, but not yet. I would like to dream it a little longer just for me.

The garden outside the windows is very quiet and full of grass. There's nothing on the grass – *nothing* – but at the back of the garden there's a tree which I go to say hello to every day. Its leaves have fallen off, but they'll come back.

Behind the garden is a field with a scarecrow, which I also talk to from time to time. It doesn't say anything, but that doesn't stop it from listening. The farmer came to take it away, but agreed to leave it because I asked him to. He smoked a pipe. I liked that. The next time I went to say hello to the scarecrow, it had a pipe.

Perhaps we'll have snow soon.

There's also a Christmas tree here, but it's nothing like the Christmas tree at the Head because it's standing on the floor and the decorations are colourful. I'll need time to get used to that.

I'll also need time to get used to there being so much space.

When the lady and I have finished talking and writing, I usually go to my room. I like sitting there, reading or sewing or looking at the ant in the amber.

I also like turning over my hourglass and staring at it. It's incredible how much sand can trickle through that small neck when you just give it time.

*Things take the time they need*, the lady says.

I wonder whether it shouldn't be *Time takes the things we took*. I've got plenty of time, but I haven't got very many things now.

I would like to know how many hourglasses of time time had to take before the small piece of resin turned into that small piece of amber with the ancient ant inside it. It exists, the ant. Because I can see it. So even though you're dead, can you still be present? It must be so. After all, I was still alive, although I was dead.

I can also see Mum. She hangs on the wall over my bed.

I've stopped being angry at them for taking away my dagger. I was allowed to keep *Robin Hood*. And my teddy bear, fortunately, although everyone says it stinks. I think it has a nice smell. Of the forest.

Roald has been here with a picture of Mona Lisa. As far as I can tell, it has been on show in another country and used to be very famous, but now it hangs here. He's right that she smiles just like Mum. They hang next to each other, Mum and Mona Lisa. Mum is nicer, I think. I've almost forgotten that she grew so big.

Almost.

I miss her. But whenever I pull out a letter from the green file and read what she wrote to me, it's a little bit like talking to her. Then I reply as best I can and put her letter back. One day, when I've read all of them, I'll probably start again, so that we can keep talking. There are so many things I want to tell her.

Sometimes I fetch a book from the common room and read it aloud to Mum and Mona Lisa. I'm not sure if Mona Lisa is listening, but at least she's looking at me wherever I sit in the room. I know that Mum is listening. She's the best listener.

They've told me that everything on the Head burned to the ground. It's not very sad because soon new things will grow, small trees – and new grass and new flowers. Everything comes back. Even the animals. One day my uncle Mogens will build a house up there, he says, and once I'm finished here, I'll go and live with him. So I, too, will be coming back.

Mogens is Dad's big brother. They don't look very much alike, but I like him all the same because I can feel that he really loved Dad. He seems nice, but also a bit odd. For instance, he keeps talking about how he has invented a clever Christmas-tree stand which you can buy in every shop. I haven't got the heart to tell him that it's a much better idea to hang your Christmas tree from the ceiling. And that that costs nothing at all.

The lady with the white name badge is also nice. She leaves me alone whenever I ask her to, and she lets me sit with my teddy, as long as I don't sit too close to her. It says 'Else' on her name badge, just as it would have done on my granny's name badge – that is, if she'd had one. I'm going to need time to get used to calling her Else, but that's quite all right, she says. Things take the time they need.

Carl is no longer quite as sad as he was when we first got here.

And, yes, the container went up in flames, along with everything else. It means that my baby sister's coffin burned as well. It's OK, though, because I managed to take the most important things with me. I have them right here. The drawing and the hourglass and *Robin Hood* and the ant in the amber.

And Carl.

And my baby sister, too. You see, on the day it all happened, I had just finished sewing her inside my teddy bear. That's why it smells of resin.

But we won't tell anyone about that.